DOUBLE DELIGHT

*To my Nephew &
His family,
Michael*

PATRICIA N. RICHARDS

Patricia N. Richards

PUBLISH AMERICA

PublishAmerica
Baltimore

First printing

All characters in this book are fictitious, and any resemblance to real persons, living or dead, is coincidental.

PublishAmerica has allowed this work to remain exactly as the author intended, verbatim, without editorial input.

Hardcover 978-1-4512-7327-4
Softcover 978-1-4512-7326-7
PUBLISHED BY PUBLISHAMERICA, LLLP
www.publishamerica.com
Baltimore

Printed in the United States of America

I would like to dedicate this book to my husband, Jim.
has been my inspiration, my help when the computer ar
don't get along, and of course my better half. I love you n.
sweet, patient husband. Thank you.

PROLOGUE

Early, clear mornings were always Rochelle's favorite time of day. Birds trilled their lovely tunes, while flying from one branch of a leafy tree to another. Rochelle wondered which was more beautiful, the flowing radiant, reddish orange colors of sunrise…or the calming glow of sunset, especially as it brings out the fabulous tones of the great Grand Canyon she was standing by. As she jogged on at a rather slow pace, her sister's image came to mind, and she hoped her sister really wasn't coming down sick with a cold, or worse, the flu. There were so many things they wanted to do and see while in this exquisite place. Maybe by staying in bed this morning, after taking the medicine she had given her sibling, she would at least try to catch the common illness before it developed into a worse condition.

The sun rose leisurely over the canyon, bringing out the resplendent shades of the rugged walls in copper, golden yellows and ember hues enhancing the spectacular view. What a breath taking place to vacation with millions of moments of splendor to grasp. All the picture postcards she had previously seen could never begin to portray the magnificent beauty and awesome vastness of this World Wonder. Last night's weather report forecast that clouds might possibly bring showers into the area. But now Rochelle enjoyed the silence of the dawn, and once in a while acknowledged another jogger with a wave of her hand.

Time was swiftly passing by, she noticed after glancing at her watch. She would be late getting back to the cottage, if she didn't hurry up her pace. As soon as she changed direction, she was startled to glimpse a rather large cat some thirty or forty feet down a ravine to her left. Although the animal didn't appear threatening, in fact it didn't even acknowledge her existence as it forged for food, Rochelle still couldn't help but feel a slight sense of anxiety. She had read the best thing to enact if encountered by a wild animal is to stand still and not run. However, that was not the natural instinct to surface in her mind at the moment.

Slowly, Rochelle began to back away, hoping to get out of the animal's sight before its range of smell picked up her scent. Unfortunately, she tripped over a log, causing her to fall backward. A broken branch had caught her shoe, twisting her ankle. When she tried to get up, the pain became excruciating. After glancing in the direction where the cougar had been forging for food, she found the animal no where in sight. Relieved, she began to crawl, trying every once in a while to get up, only to fall back to the rocky ground because of the pain.

Before Rochelle realized it, she had crawled too close to the edge of the canyon…falling over the side. Her screams of despair went unheard, intensifying the threatening mishap. Frantically, while falling down the side of the canyon, she grabbed for limbs of bushes and trees, while being scraped by large jutting stones lurking along the wall, finally grasping onto a branch that quickly gave way. Even though it was only a matter of seconds, the terror of the fall seemed an eternity for her, ending in an abrupt thud…then…nothing.

CHAPTER ONE

Tears welled up in her eyes, while Dawnelle gazed out over the mighty Grand Canyon. Clouds slowly drifted in, hanging low and gray concealing the magnificent scenery from view. But the landscape wasn't uppermost in Dawnelle's thoughts. Not this time anyway. Oh, yes, seeing the awesome renowned canyon was part of the reason why her and her sister, Rochelle, had come to Arizona after graduating from the University of Washington. They planned this trip after their parents presented them with an expense paid vacation as part of their graduation present…along with a fantastic new, red sports car.

In her recollection, the excitement of making the decision to spend the summer traveling the southwestern part of the United States, before joining the work force in the fall, filled their thoughts. Both young women had been promised employment in their father's cosmetic company in the Seattle area, after returning from their travels. They had often visited the big plant, and was always excited about the day they could be a part of their parents business.

How obvious it was to whomever observed the devotion of the Collins family. The girls were born prematurely, joined at the hips at birth, and nearly died of the intricate surgery and other complications some twenty-two years ago. Their parents, Grant and Leslie Collins, had accepted the fact that they were not able to have additional children. Instead, they felt very blessed with the beautiful identical twins they did conceive, and watch grow into fine young women.

They both had long blond hair, dark brown eyes, and pale unblemished skin. The girls loved to tease their parents and enjoyed playfully giving them a hard time, thinking of different ways to confuse their Mom and Dad, when they couldn't tell them apart.

During the developing years, the girls grew inseparable. They seemed to think alike in so many ways: their choice of clothes, food, entertainment, etc. When one would catch a bug, it wasn't long until the other would become ill. In high school they found they often chose the same classes, friends, and even liked the same boys, usually amazing each other, and always ending up laughing good naturedly over their choices. Sometimes they would trade classes just to see if they could fool the teachers, which they always did. By the time they entered college, they had decided it was time to try going each their own way. Dawnelle chose subjects in chemistry and biology, hoping to help her father develop new cosmetics and perfumes. Rochelle majored in business and management courses. In a sense this showed a difference from their childhood plans. Still, both wanted to work for their father's company.

A week after graduation and the lavish party given by their parents, the girls anxiously packed their luggage and waved good-bye to their parents, promising to keep in touch at least once a week by phone and e-mail.

The lodge at Crater Lake located high in the Cascade Mountains of Oregon was the place of their first night's rest. In her thoughts, Dawnelle could see the tiny chipmunks begging to be fed by willing visitors, then scampering along the road as it edged along the sunken lake. Patches of snow still could be seen in the shadows of tall evergreens. The sunny sky reflected its brilliant blue into the ice-cold waters of the obscure lake. An exhilarating ride in a small boat the following morning took them around Wizard Island located inside of the sunken lake. A ranger had explained how so many years ago the volcanic mountain had erupted, blowing off its top, leaving a mighty crater in the middle, which through the years filled from melting snow and rain causing the lake to take on a brilliant blue color. Ultimately, it became known as the beautiful blue Crater Lake. This was only the start of picture taking with their new digital cameras.

They drove on the next day.

While driving through the mighty giant redwood forest in northwestern California, taking many photographs, comparing their human size with the huge trees, saying hello to the huge statue of Paul Bunyan and his 'partner' the big blue ox, buying souvenirs at the many gift shops, and at times overlooking rugged inlets along the Pacific Ocean, added to the splendor of their drive south.

A few days later, after crossing the impressive Golden Gate Bridge, several hours were spent browsing the many interesting shops at Fisherman's Wharf. They even took a tour of the historic Alcatraz Prison. They found it fun to "share" a prison cell with one Clint Eastwood was supposed to have used in a movie. Later they rode a trolley to the center of bustling down town San Francisco. This is where they stood in line to buy tickets for a musical production, when a man had come up to them selling "better seats at a great price." They had been warned about "scalpers," so they turned him down. They laughed once inside, when they found the tickets they had purchased led them to the last row in the balcony, and had to use binoculars to see the show. At least the theater was near their hotel.

The twins had spent a couple of days in southern California joining the crowds at Disneyland and California Adventure, and were photographed with Mickey and his friends. Another day was spent at Knotts Berry Farm, and another at a wax museum. While at Universal Studios they learned some of the tricks in creating a movie. Both were thrilled to be chosen from the audience to participate in making a movie scene. After finding a lovely motel overlooking the swelling waves of the Pacific, they enjoyed several days relaxing and sunning on one of the irresistible public beaches near Malibu.

Dawnelle almost smiled through her tears as the sweet memories came alive in her thoughts. They were having such a wonderful time. But now an uneasy sense of concern for her sister plagued her mind. Sometimes she wished that strong sensitivity wasn't so visible. Yet it usually proved true.

Rochelle had left their cozy log cabin early that morning alone for her jog, only because Dawnelle felt she might be coming down with a cold, and had decided to sleep just a little bit longer instead of joining her sister for their usual morning run. She had told Rochelle to go on without her, and promised to join her for a late breakfast at the restaurant they had been accustomed to while at the Canyon.

Now, one o'clock had come and gone, but Rochelle had not returned. Where could she be? It wasn't like her sister to not let her know if she had altered their plans. Besides, she would have wanted to shower and change into different clothing after jogging before going to the restaurant. Something must be wrong, Dawnelle surmised. But what should she do?

With an uneasiness pricking her mind, Dawnelle wiped the tears from her face and trudged the short distance back to the cottage from where she had gone to check and see if her sister had returned. Still no Rochelle was there.

Both girls had delighted in the small cabin. It had a stone fireplace to the left of the entrance enhancing the rustic log walls. Twin beds occupied the area on either side of the fireplace with an adjoining door leading to a white tiled bathroom. A comfortable sofa ornamented in southwestern design, faced the fireplace at the other side of the room, adding a casual atmosphere while dividing the room from the modest kitchenette.

Dawnelle sat down at the table in the kitchen area and wrote her sister a note just in case she came back, explaining she would return in a few minutes, and asked her to please not leave until they talked. Then Dawnelle found the map of the area given to them when they checked in, located the Ranger Station on the map, and decided to report her sister as missing.

When Dawnelle reached the Ranger Station she wasn't sure what to say. Was she premature in thinking something may have happened to her sister? Still, she didn't know what else to do. Inhaling a deep breath, she stepped out of the red sports car and walked up to the door and entered the office of the Ranger Station. A man in the usual dark green uniform sat at a desk with his back to the entrance. He turned just as Dawnelle closed the door and glanced in her direction, nodded at her attendance, then he turned back around to finish his conversation on the phone.

Dawnelle couldn't help but overhear the ranger repeat something about sightings of a cougar being reported somewhere in the vicinity. A lump began to form in her throat, because of the rangers one-sided conversation that caused an anxious feeling to surge through her entire body. The ranger glanced her way, gave a nod an mouthed, "I'm almost finished," then hurriedly turned his chair back toward the window where he hoped she couldn't decipher what he was saying.

She wasn't sure whether she wanted to hear anymore. Yet...maybe she should.

Soon the conversation was over and the man in uniform turned and asked if he could be of any assistance. Tears began to well up in her eyes once again, but she managed to keep them in tact.

"My name is Dawnelle Collins," she looked at the man. "Uh, I'd like to report my sister missing," then they came...those uncontrollable tears. Why couldn't she restrain them in front of this stranger? Quickly, she turned her head away.

"Please sit down, Miss Collins," he gestured to the chair across from the desk. "It is Miss?" He questioned. The young woman nodded, yes. "How long has your sister been missing?" He reached for a tablet and pen.

"She left the cottage to go jogging about five this morning, but hasn't returned. The clock struck 2:00 p.m. I usually go with her, but I wasn't feeling well so I stayed in bed. We were going to have breakfast together as soon as she come back. But...but...she hasn't returned, and...oh, sir, I'm worried something has happened to her," Dawnelle's hands began shaking as she kept wiping the tears from her eyes.

"There, there, Miss," the ranger handed her a box of tissues. "I'm sure it's not as bad as it appears. Maybe she struck up a conversation with some of the friendly people in the park and has forgotten about the time," he tried to reassure her, but thought to himself that eight or so hours did seem rather a long time to not at least make an account to her sister.

"I'll need some information about her. Name. Description. If you have a photo of your sister, that would be helpful," the man was very soft spoken and kind.

Dawnelle reached for her purse, found a photograph of Rochelle in her wallet, and handed it to the ranger.

"Uh, sorry. This is a picture of you, ma'am," he offered it back to her.

"No," she smiled. "It's Rochelle. We're twins."

"Hmm, same long tawny hair and large brown eyes. Very lovely. You're identical," he stated. His mouth made an upturned sweep as he looked up, causing her to blush. It was then Dawnelle noticed how dark blue were his eyes.

"Yes. Except for our hidden scars, we've been told it's difficult to tell us apart. Er, do you think you can help, Sir?" Dawnelle wanted to get back to the reason she had come.

"I'll get a team together, and we'll start a search right away. You'd better stay at the cottage in case she shows up."

"But...I'd like to help," Dawnelle pleaded.

"Right now I think it best you go back to the cottage. Your sister might return at any time. Someone will be in touch with you the minute we have any news." Those deep blue eyes and strong jaw were very insistent, when Dawnelle began to open her mouth to protest once more. Instead, she said that she would go back to the cabin and wait...however, anxiously.

He arose from his chair and gently, taking her elbow, walked her to the door. "Please try not to worry, Miss Collins. I'm sure we'll find your sister real soon. My name is Ranger Taylor. If you should need to get a hold of me, don't hesitate. I'll give you my cell phone number," as he wrote it down, then handed her the paper with his number on it. "Please call this number to let us know if she should return to the cabin."

CHAPTER TWO

Time passed so slowly. The warm sun had begun its decent, releasing streams of coral tones spreading across the evening sky. Still no word had come about Rochelle. *"No more sitting around waiting,"* Dawnelle decided, as she thought to herself. Too much time had already elapsed without hearing some kind of news. Like it or not, Dawnelle could stay cooped up in the tiny cottage no longer. After grabbing her jacket, she hurried on back to the Ranger Station.

The ranger sat at his desk as if he'd never moved, reading some papers, feet propped up on one corner, which he quickly removed when she entered.

"Yes, ma'am. What can I do for you?" He asked, eyeing her as if for the first time.

"I spoke to you this afternoon about my sister," she felt somewhat confused when the expression on his face appeared to show no comprehension to what she was talking about." I reported her missing. Surely you remember, don't you?" She spoke with some irritation seeping through.

"I'm sorry, ma'am. I've been out of the office all day, searching for a cougar…"

"Searching for a cougar! What about my sister? She's more important than some stupid ol' animal!" Dawnelle's voice became quite sharp, unable to control her irritation.

"Wait a minute," the ranger raised his hand to calm the woman. "Cool down…"

"Cool down!" She interrupted. "Cool down? I'm suppose to cool down when you promised you'd form a search party and look for my sister. Now, you sound as if you don't even remember my reporting her missing!"

"I haven't been in the office until about an hour ago…" he started to explain, but was thwarted by Dawnelle's pounding a fist on his desk and glaring him straight in the eye.

"What kind of a bimbo do you think I am? What in the world is going on here? I demand an explanation!" her voice roared. She could never remember feeling such anger before.

A glint of humor shown in the man's eyes, when he began to speak again, "If you'll give me a chance, I will be glad to explain." His voice became more firm, "Now, sit down. Please!" Dawnelle continued to stand, glaring at him, then with a heavy sigh, reluctantly situated her body in the chair he pointed at. She took out a tissue from her pocket to blow her runny nose. She crossed her arms in disgust, "Well? I'm listening. And sitting," she growled, her features followed suit. "This had better be good."

"I am Ranger Taylor. Lance Taylor. My brother is Lyle Taylor. Lyle works the early shift when I work nights. We trade shifts monthly. We're both volunteer rangers, and run a helicopter business for our income. Anyway, you probably talked with my brother about your sister."

A bright red quickly dispersed across Dawnelle's face,

"You're twins? Identical," she stated as a fact, barely lifting her eyes. She then understood. With a groan, and in an apologetic manner, the word "Sorry" managed to squeak forth from her mouth.

"Correct, about the identical twins. As for the "stupid animal," his voice almost chuckled, "They usually are harmless unless cornered, hungry, or if they think their young might be in danger. But we can't take any chances. A cougar can be very dangerous in this area with so many visitors to the park. Some people like to try to feed wild animals, even though infatically warned not to. Others even find pleasure in antagonizing them. They have been known to attack a human," his expression became more serious. "Now about your sister."

"Rochelle, my twin sister…identical," she emphasized 'my twin' and 'identical' with a faint smile, "has been missing since early this morning. We planned to get together for breakfast after she returned from jogging, but she hasn't come back. I'm very worried that something has happened to her."

"You have that sixth sense we twins seem to be blessed with?" The ranger showed a knowing affirmation on his face. He searched through some of the papers on the desk. "Here. This must be what you are talking about. Would your sister's name be Rochelle Collins, and yours…?"

"Dawnelle. Yes, sir," she stared up at him with hope in her eyes. "Do you know anything? I mean is there any news?"

"Lyle left a note explaining he had organized a search team. He is evidently still out looking for your sister, since I haven't seen him all day. I'm sorry. That's all the information I have."

Tears once more began to form in Dawnelle's eyes, as she quickly looked down at her trembling hands.

"He'll keep up the pursuit until they find her," his voice

clearly shown sympathy. "Lyle is good at his job," he tried to reassure the young woman.

"What about the cougar? What if the cougar…ohhh, nooo," tears were streaming down her cheeks as if a faucet had broken.

"Let's not compound the problem by worrying about the cat. I'm sure there's no connection at all," yet as hard as he tried, the inflection in his voice didn't portray a real confidence. "I saw signs of a cougar in my earlier tracking today. The animal may already have wandered off and is out of the area by now," although he rather doubted it.

Dawnelle reached for another tissue from the box on the desk, gave the ranger a look, he gave her a nod of approval, then she blew her nose and said, "I feel so helpless. Isn't there anything I can do to help?"

The ranger started to say something, then hesitated, "I think I know how you must feel. If the search party hasn't found her by dark, they will have to call off the search until daylight. It's much too dangerous to pursue the hunt in the canyon after dark. I'll go out with them again at dawn. If you'd like to come along, be here at the Ranger Station by five in the morning." He looked at her shorts and tank top, "Be sure to wear sensible clothing and good walking shoes. The terrain can get rough."

"Thank you, Sir. If Rochelle hasn't returned by morning, and I surely hope she has," she sighed, "I will certainly be here. And, Mr. Taylor, please forgive my burst of anger. It's just…I've been so worried. I usually don't allow my temper to be aroused so impetuously."

"Of course. I understand," a gentle smile crossed his lips, as he gazed directly into her dark brown eyes with the same deep blue intensity as his brother's.

For some strange reason Dawnelle's heart skipped a beat. This man truly was handsome, she realized. And even through her exhibition of anger, he had been kind. She swallowed hard, as she finally tore her eyes from his probing ones.

"I, I'd better get on back to the cottage," she rose from the chair. "Again, thank you, Sir."

His tall, lean body stood and walked her to the door, "If I hear any news at all, you'll be the first to know. Oh, by the way, which cabin are you staying in?"

"'The High Trail,' number seven."

"Well, at least that's supposed to be a lucky number," a flickering gleam extended across his face. She felt he was teasing to persuade her to feel better, so she reciprocated with a demure smile, then left.

The cottage appeared dark and lonely with no sign of her sister. "Oh, please dear God, take care of Rochelle," she prayed softly, while walking to the refrigerator where she reached for a carton of milk, poured a glass to the brim, took a sip, then plopped down on the sofa. Although she hadn't eaten all day, hunger pangs were not apparent, but the milk did taste refreshing as she swallowed a couple aspirins with the drink.

It would be a long night, she suspected. She still didn't feel great, but hopefully, she'd feel better tomorrow, and Rochelle would be here.

CHAPTER THREE

Her thoughts had been provoking all kinds of havoc with her mind. She had been thinking back to her childhood days, recalling the time she and her sister had been racing with their bicycles when Rochelle's bike struck a rock, causing her to flip over the handlebars, luckily landing on a grassy knoll. Although knocked out for a few seconds, she came to. Dawnelle thought her sister was teasing because her voice was slurred, and she acted rather strange. Finally Rochelle remembered what had happened and began laughing about the mishap, both very thankful for no serious injuries.

A knock at the door startled Dawnelle.

But with her confused mind, she went on thinking.

There were other times, too, since competition in games and sports, each trying to outdo the other in an intense yet competitive way, became a real venture. Their parents had instilled in the siblings the fascination of challenge, but also how important it was to learn good sportsman-ship and how to lose gracefully. Dawnelle could almost audibly hear her sister yelling, "I'll get you next time," after each defeat, grinning like a silly clown with that mischievous beam in her eyes, knowing the 'next time' Rochelle would truly be even more eager for an invitation to a challenge.

But what about her now? Was she all right, or…?

Another LOUD knock on the door brought Dawnelle out of her unsettled reverie. Hoping it might be news, she quickly rose from off the sofa and slung open the door. Two tall rangers stood at the entrance. Neither one of their features gave her a clue as to what information they were bearing.

"Miss Collins, may we come in?" one of the men spoke, then gave a heavy sigh.

"Yes, of course. Please come in. Sorry for not answering right away." She stood aside, as they walked toward the sofa she had gestured with her hand for the men to sit down in. Dawnelle placed herself in a matching chair opposite them.

Anxious to hear what they had to report, the three began to speak all at once.

"I'm sorry," she apologized for her interruption. "Please do fill me in on any news you may have."

One of the men responded, "I wish I could say we have good news for you, but regretfully we have been unable to find your sister."

Dejectedly, fearful, and in tears, Dawnelle lowered her head down toward the floor momentarily raising it, her teeth clawing nervously at her lower lip, "You're not giving up are you?" Her eyes expressing what her voice was pleading, as she shook her head to the negative, "Please, oh please don't give up." Those tears began to fall again.

"Of course we aren't giving up," the other man quickly answered. "Like I told you earlier, it's too dangerous to search after dark. But we will have a team out first thing in the morning, and you're welcome to join us at five am."

"Yes. Yes, I want to."

The men rose to leave. They seemed to be as anxious about finding the sister as Dawnelle was.

Dawnelle thanked them for all their efforts so far, and assured them that she would be at the Ranger Station the following morning.

Every hour on the hour, it seemed, Dawnelle had checked the clock for the time, each time checking the wake up call setting. Slowly, like counting sand being released within an hour glass, the darkness turned into daylight. Wasting no time when the alarm shrilled its noisy get-up-call, she showered, dressed in her jogging outfit, gulped down a glass of orange juice, and was out the door. Disappointment set in when she found the door locked and no one at the Ranger Station.

"Oh, no. Did they leave without me?" She voiced her thoughts out loud.

Only a few clouds drifted slowly across the heavens. Dawnelle could tell, as she glanced upward to the sky that the sun was trying to squeeze through the clouds, then inspected the area about her. A moment later a Bronco with a National Park sticker arrived. The two rangers got out, waving a greeting in her direction.

"You're early, ma'am,' one spoke cheerfully.

"I might as well have spent the night here, since I didn't sleep much," she stated. She hadn't taken time to apply make-up to hide the dark circles under her dark eyes. A bright yellow scarf tied her unruly hair into a ponytail.

"We need to get a few things from the office, then we'll be on our way. Would you like to help spot for me in the helicopter, or track with Lyle and the others by mule?"

"I've never ridden in a helicopter before, but I'd like to give it a try," Dawnelle's adventurous spirit showed through.

"Fine. I'll be just a moment," Ranger Lance Taylor replied.

A few more volunteers arrived to help with the search, while the two rangers gathered their necessary supplies stored inside the building. Dawnelle introduced herself and thanked the two men and a woman for helping in the search. They informed her that they were genuinely glad to volunteer their services. The middle-aged couple proceeded to give their names as John and Glory Barton, that they lived in the area, and knew the canyon as well as anyone could. Dawnelle's sensation of hope increased, as she learned the other man was a close friend by the name of Darrell, and often helped in searching for lost visitors to the park.

The Taylor rangers joined the group momentarily, arms loaded with gear for the helicopter parked in a spot behind the Ranger Station.

"We'll be on our way shortly," Lance Taylor called out to her.

Soon the two men returned from gathering the team together. They discussed the plan that had been formulated by the rangers. The three men and the woman along with Ranger Lyle would ride the sure-footed mules, making two teams. One would travel the trail down and alongside the canyon walls, the other would search on top of the canyon. Ranger Lance and Dawnelle would search from the helicopter. Each team would report back to the Ranger Station by radio every thirty minutes until noon, if they hadn't found the missing person earlier.

Once inside the helicopter, strapped in, a helmet on her head and a device for speaking at her mouth, the vehicle quickly raised off the ground, leaving Dawnelle's stomach lingering somewhere in the depths below. The anticipation of the search and initial ride in a helicopter summoned alien sensations to capture her divided emotions. She glanced over at her companion. His competent hands were guiding the machine with knowing precision. When he turned his head in her direction, noticing the knuckles on her hands were white from grasping so tightly to the arms of the chair, he released a smile and asked, "Are you okay?"

"I'm fine," she uttered falsely into the mike.

He grinned, knowing the truth.

"Riding in a helicopter is a lot of fun once you get the hang of it. I'll try not to frighten you too much."

"Thanks. I guess I am a wee bit uneasy. I do hope we can find Rochelle soon. I haven't called our parents yet. It would just worry them. But if we don't find her today, I'll have to let them know she's missing."

He nodded in agreement. "You and your sister are very close, aren't you?"

"Yes. Inseparable. That's why I feel something terrible has happened to her. We share everything with each other. I know she would have told me before, if she would have left the area."

"Here. Take these binoculars and adjust them to your eyes for better viewing. Let me know if you spot anything we should investigate," Lance said.

Dawnelle's stomach soon calmed down, as her mind as well as her eyes began to focus on the reason for this imperative experience. She had never been one to allow despondency or grief linger for very long. The time had come for her to rely on God's protection for her sister, and seek His guidance for direction. Closing her eyes and mouthing a prayer, she felt the loving sense that God's guiding hand would lead them in the true direction.

Her mother's favorite saying came to mind, "Sometimes you have to climb a mountain to appreciate the view."

"Well, Lord, you gave me a mountain, a rough one to climb. But with your help, we're going to be successful and claim the climber's reward."

After searching every deep narrow gorge as close to the canyon walls as safety would allow, Lance turned the machine back around in the direction they had come. The team on the backs of mules following the trail to the floor of the canyon had been spotted a time or two along the way. They kept in touch with both teams by the radio transmitter. Conversation grew sparse with each passing hour, while being preoccupied in their own penetrating thoughts.

"Wait! Over there. I see something on that ledge," Dawnelle cried out elated.

Lance strategically flew the helicopter closer to where Dawnelle pointed. Something red and bulky became more visible on what Lance knew as the old trail that had partially washed away several years before during a turbulent storm.

Dawnelle kept the binoculars focused on the object, "It's a body…a…a person. Rochelle wore a red jogging outfit yesterday. It must be her," the words blurted from her mouth, desperate for hope. "But…she's…not moving."

Immediately Lance called on the radio to both teams, giving them the location of the victim, while directing the craft as close as practical to the sight.

Several minutes went by before Lyle and Darrell appeared at a distance on their mules. They dismounted their animals and with the expertise of craftsmen cautiously maneuvered their harnessed bodies along the rocky ledges of the steep canyon wall. Loose rocks gave way under their feet. Eventually, they reached the body.

During the time they were getting to the body, Lance had lowered a metal basket fastened by cables through the opening in the door of the helicopter. Quickly. Gently. The body was carefully secured, strapped and lifted carefully in the device. Then Lance raised it capably and gently into the hovering craft. Dawnelle clung to her chair in anticipation, praying the victim was her sister and that she was alive. The two rescuers were helped back up the canyon by rope and their strong mules, guided by the other two rescue team members who had arrived on the scene.

The minute Dawnelle judged it safe enough to manipulate her torso back to where the basket holding the rescued figure was situated, she found indeed it was a bruised and battered Rochelle with small broken branches clinging here and there to her ripped jogging outfit. Fervently she checked the victim for a pulse, both at her neck and at the wrist.

"She's barely breathing, but it is Rochelle and she is alive," she called out to the pilot.

"We're going to head for the hospital in Flagstaff," he acknowledged, then transmitted to the other members of the team the decision.

Dawnelle sat beside her sister, gently stroking her hand and forehead, softly speaking words of encouragement until Lance mentioned there was a blanket under the seat she was sitting on. She quickly found it and wrapped it gently around her sister. A short time later Lance was landing the chopper on top of the hospital on the landing pad designated especially for helicopters. He had radioed ahead he would be bringing in an injured patient. Orderlies with a stretcher were waiting to transport their victim to the emergency room. A nurse directed

Dawnelle to the registrars office. She went reluctantly, not wishing to leave Rochelle.

After giving the necessary information, she found Lance waiting for her in the waiting room with a cup of coffee. He smiled, taking her hand into the warm pressure of his. "I have a feeling Rochelle is going to be all right," he spoke soothingly.

A tear fell down her cheek, "You've been so very kind. I don't know how to thank you enough for what you, your brother, and the others have done for us."

"All in a day's work," Lance grinned.

"No. It's so much more than that. We'll be indebted to you always." Danielle said.

A nurse came to the visitors waiting room at that moment, "Miss Collins? The doctor would like to see you now."

Lance and Dawnelle quickly followed the nurse to the emergency room. The elderly doctor took her outstretched hand, when she introduced herself, acknowledged Ranger Taylor as if he knew him.

"Your sister will recover just fine. She has some broken ribs, a badly sprained ankle and will be sore from the scrapes and contusions received from the fall, as well as being exposed to the elements over night. I must say, she's a mighty lucky young woman. I would like to keep her in the hospital overnight for observation. She does have a slight concussion, but has regained consciousness and is asking for you."

"Oh, thank you, doctor. May I see her now?" Dawnelle asked.

"Sure. Just try to keep her calm. She'll need to rest for a few days. I'd like to see her again next week," the doctor replied.

"That would be fine," Dawnelle felt ecstatic, giving the doctor and the ranger a hug, then hurrying to Rochelle's bedside. The doctor and ranger grinned at each other.

Rochelle's eyes were open, but she appeared groggy, apparently from the medication she had been given. When she saw Dawnelle, a wide grin spread across her face.

"Hi, Dawn. Where have you been?"

"Hi, Shell. My! Have you ever given me a scare. Don't you ever do that again!" She stated emphatically, then started grinning and crying all at the same time. Her emotions released all the tension that had been building up over the past couple days. Dawnelle tried to hide her sobbing and excitement with one of Lance's hankies.

"I'm so sorry, honey. It just all happened so quickly, and I really thought it was the end for me," Rochelle's eyes were shedding tears now. They held hands and expressed joy through their tears.

"Everything's okay, Sis. Please don't cry. The doctor informed me to keep you calm. He might make me leave if I upset you. He did say that you're going to be fine. Sore, but fine. I should be able to take you back to the cottage tomorrow. We'll just relax and be lazy. In the meantime I'll be here. You need to rest and get well." Dawnelle hugged her sister as best she could, and kissed her forehead.

The doctor came in the room, "We're going to transfer Rochelle to a private room now. Why don't you get some lunch, Miss Collins, while we get her settled, then come back in about an hour."

Dawnelle noted the hour. Having no breakfast made her stomach start to growl. Then realizing she hadn't eaten anything for the last couple days, she felt starved.

"Sounds good. Thank you, Doctor." She gave her sister a gentle hug, then waved goodbye, and walked out into the hallway where she found Lance waiting.

"Ranger Taylor, I'd like to take you out for lunch," she looked at the ranger cheerfully.

"Wel-l-l, I am hungry. You think you can afford it?" He joshed.

"Since you saved my sister's life, I can afford anything you're little ol' heart desires," she beamed.

"Now that might be a tall order," his teasing eyes gave her goose bumps. "But I do have one serious request."

"Yes, Sir?"

"Please call me Lance."

"Okay, Lance, if you'll call me Dawnelle."

"Suits me fine," he gently took her arm and led her out the door. "I know of an excellent restaurant, but it's down the street a couple blocks or so. Since we don't have a car, we'll need to walk."

"Sounds great. It's such a beautiful day and I do enjoy walking," The atmosphere had disappeared from one of doom into one adorned in gems. Her smile simulated a luminous rainbow turned upside down filled with precious treasures of peace, thanksgiving and a sweet release. Dawnelle felt overwhelmed with gratitude and praise. She voiced a thankfulness to God for reviving her joy and hope, for kind people with an unlimited measure of caring, and the opportunity for making new friends. And, she was hoping this handsome ranger named Lance would be willing to be a friend while they were here in Arizona.

An inviting whisper of fresh bread's scent filtered through the air in the cozy restaurant Lance had suggested. A pleasant waitress showed them to a table by a window overlooking tall evergreens and a small garden of vibrant tones of flowers in reds, yellows and blues. A bushy tailed squirrel sat poised on its hind legs consuming a morsel of nourishment before scurrying up the trunk of one of the trees. Conversation flowed easily between Dawnelle and Lance. It was the first opportunity for the two to feel relaxed and get to know each other. The hamburger and fries really hit the spot, also.

"What would you say if you and I rent a couple rooms in a motel and spend the night here in Flagstaff, then we could fly back to the Canyon tomorrow with your sister?" Lance suggested.

"After all you have done, you would do that for us?" Dawnelle's eyes sparkled in disbelief.

"I have some friends here in Flagstaff I don't have a chance to see very often. I'd like to look them up while you visit with your sister in the hospital. Maybe we could get together for dinner and a movie later on this evening, if that would fit into your plans."

"You're very kind. I would like that very much," then she added, "But your friends may want you to spend the evening with them."

"I'll tell them I already have plans," a broad smile spread across his face.

Dawnelle's heartbeat took off on an excursion. This magnificent specimen of a male figure must not realize how susceptible she was to his charms. In fact, she couldn't understand her own emotions right now. *"He was being kind. That's all,"* she thought. Her head shook, reacting instinctively, as if trying to wake up her senses.

"Did I say something wrong?" Worried features shown on Lance's face.

"Oh, no. I'm sorry," she giggled like a high school girl. "I would love to have dinner with you," quickly adding, "if Rochelle is recuperating all right. Only remember, I don't have any change of clothes with me."

"We will find a casual place. You look just fine. Are you ready to head back to the hospital?" He asked.

She smiled and said yes. Right now she wouldn't mind going any place with him…well, within reason.

CHAPTER FOUR

The remainder of the afternoon unfolded into one of relaxation and pleasure for Dawnelle and her sister. Rochelle's recovery was progressing remarkably well, Dawnelle felt certain. However, broken ribs caused some pain when moving her body in an unsuitable way, or laughing at her sister's silly jokes. Once again life was beginning to take on a normalcy of sharing and teasing, while making plans for the next few days. Rochelle suggested a "thanksgiving" dinner with turkey, dressing, and all the traditional trimmings might be an appropriate way they could express gratitude to the volunteers who had come to her rescue. Plans were being finalized when they heard a knock on the door.

"Come in," Rochelle called out.

"This doesn't sound like a room of an injured person," a teasing voice caused the two young women to look up and grin.

Aware of the dark green uniform, Rochelle said, "You must be Ranger Taylor. Dawnelle has been telling me how you and the others risked your lives to save mine. I don't know how to thank you, Sir."

"I accept your gratitude for my part, and also I'm very thankful for your surviving such an ordeal with relatively few injuries. We aren't always so fortunate in our rescue attempts," Lance spoke.

A quiet few moments seeped through, changing the relaxed mood to one of soul searching. They each realized that the incident could very well have been one ending in tragedy.

Silence was broken by the rattle of a cart outside the door. One of the hospital personnel entered the room with a cheery voice, carrying a tray of covered dishes, "Goo' day, Miss Collins.

A delicious dinner prepared especially for you, ma' fair lassie," The woman spoke with an Irish brogue, winked at the patient lying comfortably in bed, then greeted her guests amicably. "Let me raise the bed so it will be more accommodating for you to eat." The auburn haired lady placed the tray on the table and set out to adjust the bed, fluff the pillow, and move the table into position for eating, while humming an Irish tune. "Enjoy," she called out, as she flourished from the room as quickly as she had entered. The three burst into laughter at the antics of the amusing lady.

Dawnelle took the largest cover off of a dish and smelled the meat loaf and mashed potatoes smothered in gravy, "Umm, smells yummy. Let's see what else you have." The two girls inspected the rest of the dishes with jovial teasing, deciding Rochelle would survive her first meal she had had in a couple days...without the need of an antacid. Dawnelle couldn't resist reminding her sister that it was much better than the burnt offerings Rochelle had prepared last week.

Lance stood leaning against the wall, arms folded across his chest enjoying the sisterly bantering. "Would you mind if I borrow your sister for the rest of the evening? I offered to take her to dinner and a movie, if you approve," the ranger looked at Rochelle and then her sister.

"If you want me to stay, I will," Dawnelle promptly proposed.

"Of course I don't mind. I'm a big girl. Besides, I am a little tired. I'm afraid I'd fall asleep while you're here or if you stayed much longer," Rochelle snored, wrinkling her nose, pretending to fall asleep.

Dawnelle's eyes sparkled, as she glanced in Lance's direction, "Give me a few minutes to freshen up, then we can leave this sleepyhead."

Ten minutes later the ranger and the twin were waving good-bye to the patient, encouraging her to eat every tidbit of food on the tray, so she could get her strength back and be released from the hospital the following day.

"I like your sister," Lance chuckled, while they walked down the hallway to the elevator. She reminds me of you," he winked and grinned. "You two tease each other as much as Lyle and I do." A mouth full of perfect teeth became evident.

"We always have enjoyed being together. When I thought I had lost her…ohh, I don't know what we'd do without each other. I don't think we could ever get married, if the other wasn't near."

"Hmm. If the right man were to come along, he'd probably help change your mind," he smiled.

The elevator door opened. They stepped in. Lance's eyes captured hers. Both stared into the other's eyes until the door opened again, jarring their unwanted attention to the patrons and visitors desiring to enter the small domain.

Lance quickly took his companion's arm and guided her

without haste toward the hospital's entrance. When they stepped out into the sunshine, a fresh breeze caught a strand of Dawnelle's long hair, blowing it across her face.

"Do you care for Mexican food?" Lance turned to face Dawnelle and brushed the hair back, while softly touching her face.

Barely raising her eyes, her face flush, she spoke, "Very much."

"I borrowed a car from my friend. The restaurant and theater are too far away to walk to. And upon your approval, I also reserved two rooms in a premium motel closer to town. I hope you don't mind."

"That was thoughtful of you. But I insist on paying my share."

"I will relent on the motel. However, I invited you to dinner and a movie, so I'll insist on paying for them," the tone in his voice firm.

"Yes, Sir. Ranger, Sir," standing erect, Dawnelle gave him a salute, a chuckle followed. By the time they reached the car the mood had changed to one of ease. She hadn't forgotten Rochelle in the hospital, but she felt free from stress for now.

Sombreros, murals, pottery and other Mexican paraphernalia decorated the walls of the restaurant Lance had chosen. Pretty waitresses were colorfully dressed in bright tiered skirts and white ruffled blouses. Mexican music added to the atmosphere. The enchiladas, pinto beans and Spanish rice were excellently prepared with just the right amount of spices, but the "fried" ice cream really contributed that fascinating touch. They left the restaurant stuffed and in a festive mood.

Dawnelle was pleased to find the movie a comedy instead of the shoot'em up, killer—thriller that seems to plague the television, as well as theater screens. She often thought: If someone isn't shot, knifed, karate chopped, on drugs, or power hungry the television programs or movies aren't acceptable entertainment to the public now days. Yet even then, we wonder why so many in our society are troubled. Maybe we could attribute our so called entertainment as part of the reason (?)

While walking leisurely hand in hand to the car after the movie, Dawnelle breathed in the warmth from the left over rays of the sun. Looking up into the ebony sky, millions of luminous stars appeared so close she felt like reaching out and plucking one for her chest of treasures. A full moon was trying to hide its glow behind a cloud, that soon drifted ever so slowly by. High up in a tree, a robin trilled a sweet melody, even though the afternoon had drifted away.

"It's been such a lovely evening. Thank you for allowing me to share it with you," Dawnelle sighed.

"My pleasure, ma'am. It has been a long day. Are you ready to go to the motel, or would you like to stop for a soda or something?"

"We'd better be getting to the motel. I am rather tired. You probably are, too. It's been an extraordinary day with the search for Rochelle, and ending with such an enchanting evening. I imagine you're anxious to get back to the Canyon tomorrow as early as possible."

"I do need to get back to our helicopter business, as well as the ranger position. Flying is my life. Lyle and I have profited quite well flying tourists on excursions of the canyon and helping in rescues when needed. We also bring in supplies for the businesses in the area. In fact, I need to pick up some items before we leave tomorrow. As soon as Rochelle is able to travel, we'll head back."

Dawnelle found the motel room modern and luxurious.

Floral wallpaper blended nicely with the cushioned comfort of carpet, which was so plush her feet sank into its softness. The king size bed would swallow up her slender body, but looked enticingly comfortable. When Dawnelle opened the sliding glass door and walked onto her own personal veranda, she found it over-looking a pool, enhanced by lights strategically placed, adding a romantic touch. She didn't realize the moonlight dancing in her golden hair. Nevertheless, a certain man on the veranda next door noticed not only her shimmering hair, but the loveliness of the woman leaning against the veranda wall.

"Did you find the room to your satisfaction?" Lance's deep voice vied with her thoughts.

"Oh, hi. How nice to have adjoining rooms. Makes me feel safe," she smiled.

"Hmm, if she knew what I was thinking, she wouldn't feel so safe, although I'd never take advantage of her," he thought to himself, but didn't voice those thoughts aloud. "I'm glad you feel safe with me, Dawnelle. How about joining me for a swim?"

"Sorry, I don't have a swim suit."

"Uh, oh. That's right," he chuckled. "Well, how about a little stroll through the park nearby? Might help you sleep better."

"That would be nice. I'm really not sleepy...tired...but not sleepy."

They met in the hallway and walked to the exit, then across the street. Trickling sounds flowed from a fountain situated in the center of the small well lit park. A mixture of summer flowers dispersed fragrant scents through the evening air adding to the source of pleasure.

"When we get back to the canyon I hope you'll allow me to see you while you're in the area," Lance took her hand in his.

"I'd like that very much. Rochelle and I would like you, Lyle, and the other three who helped with the rescue to come for dinner as soon as she is able."

"Sounds good to me," he said.

They stopped walking, Lance turned to face his companion, taking both her hands in his,

"This may sound foolish, but I'm beginning to care for you, Dawnelle. I know we haven't known each other for very long, yet I desperately have a need to kiss you."

Their eyes met, then their lips gently touched for a time.

"I, I think we'd better get back to the motel," Dawnelle whispered, as she drew back from his embrace. "I promised Rochelle I would be at the hospital bright and early in the morning."

"Have I frightened you?" Lance asked. A worried look became visible.

"Everything is happening so fast. I've never felt like this before. Oh, I've been kissed, but…"

"My feelings are mutual. Maybe it's just the excitement of the past couple days. We'll see what tomorrow brings," his words were spoken tenderly.

They strolled hand in hand back to the motel where they said good night at Dawnelle's door. Lance didn't attempt to kiss her again, not wanting to trouble their feelings more than he already had.

CHAPTER FIVE

A sunshine patch of yellow roses appeared to reign near the pool area when Dawnelle lazily walked onto the veranda early the next morning. Puffy white clouds scattered as if just awakened from their siesta. A potpourri of fragrance permeated the softly flowing breeze with Sweet William and honeysuckle vines clinging to the wall of the motel. Someone honked a horn nearby, as if anxious to be on their way.

"Good morning," a familiar voice interrupted Dawnelle's time of solitude. "Did you sleep well?"

"Yes, very well, thank you," she couldn't disguise the glorious smile claiming her lips. Just hearing his voice tenderly touched her heart.

"Could I interest you in joining me for breakfast?"

"I'd love to join you." Dawnelle wasn't much of a breakfast eater, but she didn't want to refuse his offer. "Give me five minutes," she remarked.

They found the restaurant adjoining the motel served delicious, feather-light Belgium waffles and enjoyed their fill. It was too early to visit her sister, so Dawnelle offered to help Lance in gathering the supplies he was to take back to the businesses at the Grand Canyon Village. She also picked out a new blue pants outfit for Rochelle, since her clothes had ruined from the accident, and couldn't resist a green one for herself to wear on the trip back. Lance also needed to return the borrowed car to his friend, who lived close to the hospital.

The friend, Dawnelle learned, was another one of Lance and Lyle's rescued victim's of the area. Mr. Raye had been attacked by a mountain lion a couple years ago. He was able to survive the attack, but had to be lifted out by helicopter to the hospital in Flagstaff because of his grave condition. Although not expected to live, he pulled through and awards the credit to God and His angels: the doctors and nurses, along with Lance and Lyle Taylor. Whenever one of the Taylor men are in town, they always make it a point to check on him. For a man nearing eighty years old, they found him to be a pretty spry gentleman.

After visiting the dear man for a few minutes, Lance and Dawnelle walked leisurely to the hospital enjoying each other's company. They laughed with each other, still arriving in time to find Rochelle zealous and able to leave. The doctor had already given instructions for her continued recovery. The pleasure was obvious when Rochelle accepted the gift of a new outfit from her sister. Lance talked with the doctor and accepted Rochelle's prescription for medication along with directions for its use, while the girls changed into their new apparel.

They were both pleased when Kathleen, the Irish Lady, was the one who entered the room to escort Rochelle from the hospital in her wheelchair, insisting she take her to the helicopter. She rambled all the way in her Irish brogue about the weather, and how nice it was in America, and how friendly the people were to her. Of course she was the one so friendly. One could not help but enjoy being around her winsome character. Both girls decided they would allocate some time to visit with their new friend before leaving Arizona.

The flight back to the canyon was pleasant with completely different emotions than the flight to Flagstaff. Rochelle had adjusted to the twinge of pains she would have to endure for awhile.

"Oh, I must feel like an eagle spreading its wings for the first time." She stretched her arms, reflecting a glow of sunshine. "It's so good to be alive. Ohh, ouch…but I still have to remember I'm not healed," she giggled a little nervously to disguise the pain.

"I bought some books and magazines to read and a jigsaw puzzle to challenge us. We'll enjoy being lazy a few more days," Dawnelle informed her.

"That's my thoughtful sister. Say, have you talked with Dad and Mom yet?"

"No. I probably should have. No doubt they would have been here by now, but I didn't want to worry them until I found out you were all right. We'll call them when we get back to the cottage. You can tell them of the accident, and then they'll know you're doing okay."

"They will be upset and insist we come home," Rochelle wrinkled her nose.

"Well, you can't travel yet. As soon as you're able, we might have to head for home. Right now we're going to concentrate on your recovery. Doctor Dawnelle has spoken," she joshed.

"Yeh. You tell that to Dad," Rochelle laughed.

Time slipped away so expeditiously, they were amazed when Lance set the helicopter down on the landing pad behind the Ranger Station. He had radioed ahead, so Lyle met them with a wheelchair for Rochelle the minute he heard the chopper. She argued at first that the chair was unnecessary. Yet as soon as she put weight on her sprained ankle, the wheelchair called to her to come. At that moment Rochelle made her acquaintance with another who had assisted with her rescue. A display of astonishment shown on her face, since Dawnelle had not mentioned that Lyle was Lance's identical twin.

"My deepest gratitude to you, Ranger Taylor, for your part in my rescue," she kept staring at him. Not only was he an exquisite image of his brother, but had also risked his life for hers. "I understand you had to crawl along the canyon walls to reach me, jeopardizing your own life to save mine," she shook her head in awe. "I'll always be grateful."

"My pleasure, ma'am. But I did have help from my friend, Darrell. He's really the expert. I'm delighted to see you're considerably better than when we found you on that ledge."

"I'll drive you girls to the cottage," Lance interrupted the conversation, while Dawnelle gathered the few articles they had in the chopper.

Once in the cottage and the rangers gone, Rochelle couldn't wait to ask, "Why didn't you tell me that Lyle and Lance are identical twins. I really would have looked forward even more to coming home to our little cottage. They are sooo good looking," a broad smile spanned her features, her eyes as big as balloons.

" I wanted to watch the reaction on your face when you met him," she teased. Then Dawnelle told about the embarrassing situation of meeting both rangers at their office, when reporting her as missing and not knowing the rangers were identical twins, remembering how she had spoken so ruefully to Lance.

Three days later, after the girls had driven down to Flagstaff for the doctor's appointment and received a good report for her condition, Rochelle was curled up on the sofa following lunch, sighing and wiping her eyes. She had just finished reading another of Karen Kingsbury's latest novels. Dawnelle was content to have accomplished the feat of hooking together the last piece in the border of a two-thousand piece jigsaw puzzle.

There was a knock on the door.

"We thought it was about time to check up on you two," Lance spoke when Dawnelle opened the door. Lance and Lyle stood at the entrance dressed in denim jeans and tee-shirts inscribed with their company logo.

"Come in. Besides fighting cabin fever, we're doing great," Dawnelle's features couldn't hide the fact that she was delighted to see the familiar faces.

"It's our day off. We thought it would be nice to give you girls a change of pace. How about a movie?" Lyle suggested. "Do you feel up to it?" He glanced in Rochelle's direction.

Her eyes beamed, "Sounds wonderful. Is there a theater near by?"

"How does Phoenix sound?"

"But that's over two-hundred miles," both girls squealed, while grinning from ear to ear.

"Not so far with the chopper, and it's raring to go," Lance informed them.

Looking at each other, then at the two guys, "Why not!" They both spoke at the same instant with astonishment in their eyes.

"We'll pick you up at two. All right?" Lance winked. Both girls smiled and looked at each other grinning.

When the guys arrived to pick them up, they had changed in to dress pants and sport shirts. The girls wore similar styled floral sun-dresses with matching jackets. Dawnelle's dress favored the colors of peach. Her light blond hair was fashioned in curls on top of her head with soft twists of spirals falling from her temples, ears and neck. Dawnelle applied just enough make-up to bring out her deep brown eyes and flawless skin. Rochelle wore her hair loosely curled, flowing down past her shoulders. The bright yellows in her dress matched the carefully placed bows adorning her golden hair to help hide some scars from the accident, as well as hide, as best she could, the black and blue scars still visible on her face . She had wrapped a bandage around the healing ankle to help protect it. They, of course, used make-up purchased from their father's cosmetic factory.

Their dates scrutinized them with satisfaction, and didn't mind expressing their approval loudly.

Lyle piloted the helicopter allowing Rochelle to ride up front, while Lance and Dawnelle rode in the second row of seats.

"This is the first time to have a date pick us up in a helicopter," Rochelle exclaimed. "We might get spoiled," she grinned.

"I must admit, we use it mainly for business purposes, but we decided this is a special occasion," Lyle remarked. "We don't have the opportunity to escort two beautiful ladies all that often," he grinned and she blushed. They all adjusted the ear phones.

"Hey! What's that over there?" Dawnelle pointed.

"I'll bet that's the cougar we've been tracking. We haven't been down this far south looking for the animal, Lyle. Looks like it's heading away from the park, so shouldn't be of any danger for the guests or residents. We'd better continue to keep our eye on the animal though."

The men pointed out different sites of interest while flying over the mountainous terrain using the flight plan that Lyle had worked out. Their love of the Grand Canyon State awakened the young women's admiration for the land of many contrasts with its distinctive saguaro, exotic cactus plants, tranquil deserts and rich heritage of Indian and Mexican culture. More gorges and impressive, yet lesser canyons than the World of Wonder, are still being carved by wind and water after millions of years. Sometimes Lyle lowered the chopper closer for more excellent views among fascinating scenery of rolling rivers and various kinds of wild life. The scenery, especially around Sedona, Arizona is surrounded with red rocky mountains towering in stature surrounding the lovely tourist town.

"Sedona has been described as 'The Most Beautiful Place in America,'" Lyle proudly announced to his passengers. "Writers and artists and photographers travel from all over the world just to try to capture the beauty of this awesome place, that has been described as ' a place that looks like nowhere else.'" It was very obvious that the guys were very proud of their home state.

Their imagination soon began to fantasize, when viewing the echoing ruins of cliff dwellers, the scores of pueblos still fervent with life, the chanting and drum intonations of the modern Indians honoring gods of their fathers, looms of weavers, masters of silver and turquoise, potters of ancient designs all carrying on the arts of their ancestors and giving glimpses of an enticing past. Much of the Arizona population is Indian, they learned, many living on reservations; the largest being the Navajo in the area. Mud and log houses called hogans are still seen occasionally. The warmth from the sun still lingered in "The Valley of the Sun."

The four took advantage of the airport car rental service for the drive to the centrally located part of Phoenix, a busy modern, yet casual city. The area was convenient to shopping plazas, beautifully landscaped gardens and fine restaurants...one of which they had reservations for dinner.

After dining on Cantonese cuisine in a charming restaurant,

Dawnelle asked if the men would mind stopping to purchase some groceries before heading back to the canyon. They found a store that would be open for twenty-four hours, and decided to take advantage of their services following a movie.

"That was such a funny, yet romantic film," Rochelle mentioned to no one in particular, while leaving the theater.

"Yes. I wish they would make more movies like that," her sister agreed. "And musicals. They never make enough musicals anymore."

"Not enough action for me," Lance groaned.

"No blood and guts," grinned Lyle.

"Oh, you guys. You just don't know what's wholesome any more," Rochelle grimaced.

"Are we on our way home? If so, let's stop at the store," Dawnelle reminded them, deciding to change the subject.

They found a super market a short distance from the airport. Both girls found shopping carts and began filling them up with groceries. "You sure are hungry," one of the guys announced, teeming with amusement.

"We're planning a Thanksgiving Dinner," replied Dawnelle.

"A little early aren't you?" grinned Lyle.

"It's never too early to be thankful," Rochelle smiled.

"And when is this big occasion going to take place, and is anyone invited or are you two going to eat all this food by yourselves?" Those beaming eyes sparkled on Lance's face.

"We might invite you two. But especially Darrell and the couple who came to my rescue," the answer came teasingly from Rochelle.

"Do you suppose there's a way we could invite Kathleen, my nurse?" Rochelle thought out loud.

"Sure. You could call the hospital in Flagstaff and get her

phone number, or at least have them give her a message to call you, if that is not allowed," suggested Lance.

"But we don't have a phone number for the hospital."

"I'm sure we have it at the Ranger's Office," he responded.

Lyle filed a flight plan for the return trip to the canyon. Nearly all the way back to the cottage the topic of conversation during the flight focused on the Thanksgiving Dinner. Even the rangers were caught up in the girl's excitement. They decided to plan the dinner for the day after tomorrow, providing everyone could come.

CHAPTER SIX

A time of thanksgiving, even though it wasn't the national holiday, planning it was a time of excitement. What could be done the day before…cleaning, decorating the tiny cottage with balloons and streamers and baking pumpkin pies…was completed with gaiety and laughter. The Taylor brothers had offered to invite the other four guests with confirming results.

Shyness crept in when Rochelle actually met John and Glory Barton, and Darrell in the flesh. One doesn't often have the opportunity to meet someone who has saved your life, she thought. A sense of awe, respect, and admiration for these people who seemed to accept their part as no more than an every day occurrence swept through her being. Each one indicated pleasure to make her acquaintance, and declared with much satisfaction regarding the savory aroma of roasting turkey and dressing permeating the atmosphere. Kathleen arrived a little later than the others since she had the farthest to come.

As they gathered around to partake of the buffet meal, Dawnelle asked each one to hold hands with another, while leading them in a prayer of thanksgiving for the gift of life, new friends and the families they represented, and for all the blessings God had bestowed upon them.

She then shared, "A pastor once said, 'If God calls you to a heroic task, expect to work like a hero.' I feel you all fit that description."

Kathleen became the joy of dinner with her silly leprechaun stories of searching for pots of gold at the end of rainbows, exaggerating with her fantasies.

"Course the leprechaun only comes out at night," she went on. "Ya have to be blessed to see them. Such sly wee fellows are they, with tall black hats and long white beards. They laugh a lot, ya see, but they're awfully sneaky. Once ya've made friends with one, he'll protect ya the rest of your life. Aw, but watch out if they don't like ya. They'll rob ya blind if ya aren't careful.

"And drink! Oh, my! They'll drink more than any one person I've ever known, and they'll get in to all kinds of mischief. I've seen horse's tails tied to a fence, and when they ride off…there goes the fence. Or a leprechaun might shake a tree with a twist of his nose, and cause the squirrels to throw pine cones on top of one he dislikes, knocking him unconscious.

"Now the Unicorn, the horse with a lo-o-n-n-g horn attached to his head, is one that flies like the wind on a stormy day. He can carry the largest of men across the mountains and back in no time at'all, never touching a speck of ground. When one of these animals is put under the spell of a leprechaun, it could charge the meanest lion and win just by shooting daggers with its eyes. Or it might lie down beside a crocodile and they both fall asleep without any hassle.

"And did ya know now, if two lovers hold hands and kiss the blarney stone, they are guaranteed a long happy marriage, but only if each one holds a shamrock behind their back in their right hand?"

Kathleen became the pleasure of the celebration with her silly tales. Her eyes danced from the seeds of mischief she was spreading. They couldn't help but wonder if the lady was fabricating the tales while uttering them, or even become convinced she might be part leprechaun herself.

While the women washed dishes and cleaned up the kitchen, Darrell began strumming on his guitar he had brought. Soon everyone gathered together to sing favorite old tunes, including some Irish melodies taught by Kathleen, reminding her of another tale or two.

Millions of moments of memories later the guests began to leave expressing their gratitude for an evening of pleasure. Rochelle asked each one to give her their addresses.

Ah, tis sweet of ya ma' lovalies to invite such as me to take pleasure from a fine and delightful dinner with such nice people. The memories I'll keep tucked within ma' very own soul for always," Kathleen's words touched the hearts of the hostesses.

"The pleasure is assuredly ours." Dawnelle shook her head in agreement with her sister's spoken thoughts.

Lance and Lyle were last to leave. "What more can we say that has not already been said? You both did an outstanding job at cooking and providing a very entertaining evening." Lance took Dawnelle's hands in his.

"Everyone contributed to the evening. We're so glad for each one who come, and for what this evening represents," Dawnelle gazed into his face.

"Aw, ma' little lovely," he grinned and softly brushed his thumb over her nose then, lifted her chin and touched his lips to hers.

"Ah, umm. Sorry to interrupt such a tender caress," a

thimbleful of caring strived to cover the teasing tone being released from Lyle's mouth. "However, we'd better leave these fair ladies. The hour is very late little bro."

Rochelle stood at Lyle's side with eyes enchanted by the scene unfolding. Her sister evidently had unspoken dreams yet to be shared. What a pleasant thought. At that moment Lyle kissed her, immediately both rangers headed for their car, waving their good-byes. Rochelle stood there with her mouth open, then touched her lips so softly. Finally, she joined her sister returning their waves, watching as they drove away, while filled with an abundance of emotions peeking through. God's rhapsody of twinkling stars covered the heavens with their sweet presence. Neither wanted to interrupt the serenity of the moment.

A loud knock on the door aroused the two sleeping so soundly in their beds early the following morning. Dawnelle quickly got up after the second knock became louder. "Just a minute," she called out while grabbing her robe.

An unknown man dressed in a ranger uniform stood impatiently at the door when Dawnelle opened it, "You had an emergency call at the Ranger's Office. Your father said to return the call as soon as possible." He was thanked for the information.

Dawnelle stepped back into the room, stunned.

After overhearing the news, Rochelle quickly as possible, causing a little pain while putting on her clothes said, "I wonder what's wrong. There must be something wrong," a frown shown on her lovely face.

Dawnelle reached for their cell phone, but the battery was dead. As soon as they both could dress, they drove to the office.

Neither Lance nor Lyle were there, but they asked to use the phone anyway.

Dawnelle made the call home.

"Daddy? What's wrong?" Dawnelle asked immediately, after being connected to the number at home.

"I had to take your mother to the hospital last night. She was doubled over in pain. They don't know what's wrong, but they are running tests," his voice quivered with emotion. "Can you come home? I need you here."

"Of course, Daddy. We'll leave as soon as we get packed. We'll call every night until we get home," Dawnelle looked at her despondent sister.

Even not knowing all the facts, Rochelle knew it had to be bad news. Dad never would have called, if it wasn't important.

After sharing what little she did know, they left a note for Lance and Lyle with the ranger in the office, explaining their rapid departure and giving them their address and phone number. He assured them he would see that one of them got the note, as he reached automatically to place it in the their slot for mail.

It didn't take them long to pack, leave a note on the refrigerator that they were sorry they didn't have time to clean out the leftovers from the thanksgiving dinner, and were soon on the road heading home in their red sports car with Dawnelle driving. A mixture of feelings laden with cares: will their mother be all right, will they ever see the Taylor men again? Each thought went through their minds.

The drive home was certainly not the sweet adventure they had anticipated when planning their trip at the beginning of the summer. But then, meeting two men of their dreams only to leave them behind without seeing them before they left, had not been in their plans either. And, unfortunately, they didn't notice their note missed the slot for Lance and Lyle's mail. Instead it had landed in the waste basket immediately below. Nor did they know Lance and Lyle were called to help in an emergency. A dangerous forest fire in Southern California had broken out of control, destroying several homes and threatening more. Any available fire fighters, especially those using aircraft, were encouraged to help in bringing the fire under control. The Taylor brothers had left in their helicopter that morning just before daylight to offer their services.

The first few hours of travel for the Collins' twins had remained one obsessed in silence. Summer's sun gave them no release from the penetrating heat, although the car's air conditioner remained committed to working overtime.

Finally, Rochelle broke the stillness, "I'm getting hungry. I suppose we should find a place to eat in the next town."

"Yes. I'm sorry. I should have stopped in Needles. It's at least a couple hours to Barstow going west. We do have some cans of orange juice in the cooler behind your seat. Can you reach them or do you want me to stop?"

Rochelle managed to dig out the cans of juice without much twisting to her ribs, which helped to relieve the thirst and break the silence. Dawnelle turned on the radio and found a station playing some cheerful music. They began to share their feelings with one another. They both felt their lives had been derailed for a while, but that was not going to stop them for long. God had always been in control of their lives and they felt confident He would continue to work His wonders toward that ultimate goal He had planned for them. Rochelle voiced a prayer for confidence that their mother would be all right, their travels would be safe, and if it was in His will, they might even get to see Lyle and Lance again some day...soon.

CHAPTER SEVEN

After three long days of driving from dawn until the stars appeared, stopping only to eat, buy gas, or spend a few hours of rest in a motel, the anxious twins arrived at home in the Evergreen State. They found the two-story house dark and assumed their father was at the hospital with their mother. Each evening on the road they had called home from the motels to check on her condition, only to learn from their father that the tests had not come back yet. The most they knew about her condition was their dear mother was under medication for pain and feeling some relief.

When the young women unlocked the door and entered the kitchen, they found a note from their father on the kitchen table saying their mother was to have surgery early that morning. He would be home as soon as he knew she was out of danger and everything went well. He would explain the details when he come home.

After unpacking their clothes in their separate bedrooms and showering, they heard the garage door opening and knew their father had arrived. Both were eager for news of their mother, and ran down the stairs to meet him.

"How's Mama?" Both girls blurted out at once, as they ran into their father's outstretched arms.

"Your mother is doing fine. She's still under sedation and probably won't even remember my being there, but the doctor reported everything went well."

"What's wrong Daddy? Why the surgery?" Dawnelle asked. "She sounded all right the last time we talked with her."

"Your mother isn't a complainer, as you well know. Evidently she's had pain for some time, and finally it got so bad she couldn't keep it from me any longer. She had gall bladder surgery. The doctor found a stone an inch and a half in length, plus several smaller ones. He put them in a jar for us to see. Laughingly the doctor handed the jar to your mother, then asked if she wanted them for a souvenir. At first she protested with a positive 'No,' but ended up giving the reason for her misery to me." He took the small jar from his pocket, and showed his daughters the contents.

By week's end, the family brought Mrs. Collins home to a sparkling clean house and a bouquet of bright red roses with a huge 'Welcome Home' balloon sitting on the table with colorful steamers attached from one side of the kitchen to the other.

"Ah, to be a family again. It's so very nice to have my two beautiful daughters home. You are my children, my flowers that decorate my life," Mrs. Collins avowed teary eyed. Then she noticed Rochelle. "Oh, darling, your face. Where did you get all those scars?"

"It's nothing, Mama. I'm almost healed." She moved gingerly not wanting to reveal her ribs still hurt some. Remember, we called and I told you I had fallen," and hoped she'd never find out how close she had come to losing her life, Rochelle thought to herself.

"But you didn't tell me you were so badly hurt," the mother expressed with added concern.

"We didn't want you to worry, Mama. Really, I am fine. Let's get you well now."

"I'll have to be careful what I eat for awhile. Now that you girls are home, everything will be all right. Your dad has treated me like a child while you girls were away. I've become so spoiled. But I must say, I've enjoyed every minute of his attention," she looked at her husband lovingly and smiled.

A month has gone by since the twins come home. The Collins' household regained the normalcy they once enjoyed, and yet some of the exuberance that had always characterized the daughter's lives seemed to be lacking. Both young women had started working in their father's cosmetic business and appeared delighted to be using their skills they had been taught in college. However, something obviously bothered them. They were just not themselves. Their mother decided to confront her daughters one evening when their father worked late. She hoped to find out why the change.

"Are you girls finding your work in the cosmetic business challenging?" She began. "You know you don't have to stay in the business just because your father owns it. We both want what's best for you. We want you to do what you want to do."

"Why, Mother, what makes you think we aren't happy?" A curious expression shown on Dawnelle's face. "We've always desired to be a part of daddy's business."

"Neither one of you seem contented. Something must have happened during your travels. Please, I'd like you to feel you can share any problems you have with me. Did you two have a fallen out, or was it because of having to come back earlier than planned on account of my illness?"

"Well…while we were in Arizona we met two men. They're identical twins, Mama," Dawnelle smiled. "They were such extraordinary guys. They have a helicopter business, touring the Canyon, and volunteering as part time rangers because of the financial difficulties our National Parks are experiencing."

"Their parents had died in a terrible plane crash a couple years ago. They have an older brother and sister who are both married. With the guy's share of the insurance money, they started the helicopter business from their inheritance. Anyway, because of my accident," Rochelle said, "we got to know them and dated a couple times. Suddenly we didn't have a chance to tell them good-bye when we left. Although we did leave a note with our address and phone number with a park ranger, explaining why we needed to leave. But they have never called or tried to get in touch with us. Dawnelle and I both were beginning to care, perhaps too deeply, but evidently the feelings were not mutual. I guess we'll never see them again."

Rochelle sighed, then turned aside to wipe away the tears.

"Have you tried to get in touch with them since you've been home?" Mrs. Collins asked.

"No. We felt if they really cared for us, they would call us," Dawnelle answered.

"Besides, we don't have their phone number. As far as we know, they should have ours."

"Well, if I were you, and really cared, I would call them. You should be able to get the phone number of their business through information."

"Why didn't we think of that?" Dawnelle spoke, as her eyes beamed at her sister. "It's probably too late to find anyone there tonight, but we could get the phone number and try in the morning."

First thing early, before work the following morning, Rochelle dialed information. When she asked for the number of Taylor Canyon Tours by Helicopter a sightseeing business, astonishment spread across her face, "The number has been cancelled. They have gone out of business."

"Get a number for the Ranger Office," Dawnelle quickly suggested.

After given that number, Rochelle dialed it, and was informed that the Taylor brothers had quit their volunteer job and moved. The one answering the phone did not know them personally, nor where they had gone.

Gloom quickly set in.

"Maybe it wasn't meant to be. However, we know God wants only the best for us. True love grows, never dies. In His time you two will meet the men that God has planned for you." Mom said in a loving, caring tone.

"But, Mama. I really thought I had met him," Dawnelle shook her head sadly. This time she couldn't hold back the tears.

CHAPTER EIGHT

Summer had come and gone. Leaves on the maple trees were exchanging their colors from green to accents of gold, crimson and bronze. A slight chill in the air left one with an invigorating and refreshing feeling. Even the sunsets dispersed a more brilliant coral hue taking command of the realm above the earth. Days grew shorter.

Dawnelle had not noticed the shorter days. She had been laboring over a special formula for several weeks, and become so engrossed in striving to discover the vital ingredient necessary for her task to succeed, that many of her hours had extended into twelve and fourteen hour days. Her craft had completely absorbed her life. Now, she finally felt it was time to tell her family of the great discovery. When she walked into the family room, she found the three family members sitting relaxed listening to the Bose, soft, clear sounds of music while reading. Mom was engrossed in her favorite book of poems, Dad sat reading the Bible, while her sister was involved in a Danielle Steel novel.

"You're late again, dear," Mama Collins acknowledged her entrance. "You work much too hard. Please sit down and rest while I warm you something to eat in the microwave," her mother sympathized.

"Thanks, Mama. Sounds terrific. I just realized, I'm starved," Dawnelle hung her coat in the closet and collapsed in her favorite chair. A few minutes later Mrs. Collins brought in a tray of her favorite Mexican food.

"I believe I've created a new product, Daddy. I've been working on a new facial cream to help dissolve wrinkles around the eyes, the mouth, and to help get rid of wrinkles in other tender parts of the face. It can be colored in flesh tones and used as makeup or as a base. The ingredients are less expensive then a lot of the creams now on the market, so we can keep the cost factor down to a minimum. The average person would be able to afford to purchase our product," the excitement from Dawnelle's voice filled the room, stimulating her family's interest. They had put their reading material aside to listen to her announcement.

"To provide a product the average person can afford and buy would really be super," Rochelle encouraged, "and it wouldn't hurt business either." she shared with enthusiasm.

"Mama, I've noticed a few little wrinkles beginning to show around your eyes. I would like you to test the cream for two weeks and see if you notice any improvement to your skin. There's absolutely nothing in the cream that could harm you." Dawnelle mentioned in a meek manner.

"Me? Be your guinea pig?" Mrs. Collins scrunched up her nose and smiled. "Wel-l-l, maybe for a week or two," she grinned.

Dawnelle handed her a jar of the mystery cream. She opened it. "Umm," her mother inhaled a breath of scent. "Smells devine. Have you decided on a name for your new creation?"

Rochelle reached for the jar. After taking a whiff, she suggested, "How about 'Heavenly Delight?'"

Dawnelle rolled her eyes in a questioning manner, "I thought of 'Jewel of Disguise,'" she said, while looking at her sister's smiling eyes.

"Yeh! I like that even better," Rochelle surrendered.

"Not bad," the father agreed, as he sniffed the jar and rubbed some cream between his fingers.

"When can we proceed with our new discovery?" Dawnelle asked her father, inflecting eagerness in her voice. After all, he was the "Boss."

"Let's see what your mother looks like after a week or two," he spoke with a smile. " If she has the appearance of a woman ten years younger, we'll get started right away," her father winked at his wife. However, he exhibited much pleasure in his daughter's abilities. Although being in the cosmetic business for many years, he knew it took time and money to establish a new product. Yet casting a damper on Dawnelle's enthusiasm was the last of his intention.

Because the ingredients in the new product were considered already acceptable, no restrictions were imposed upon the company to keep them from moving forward with the processing of the new 'miracle cream' called 'Jewel of Disguise.' And, their mother loved the experimental cream she had tried.. The cream was accepted.

As time went by, both young women became involved in deciding on a satisfactory advertisement promotion through television and radio commercials, hoping to grab public attention for the up coming Christmas season.

Louis Markham, the new man in charge of advertising, insisted on using the girls in the commercials, because of their wholesome sex appeal. What a new experience. Neither one had ever thought of modeling or acting before, and this involved both. Now a new challenge had been thrust upon them. One they were not sure was to their liking. They both wondered if this was in God's will. Together they prayed many hours before accepting this challenge.

Lou was young, enthusiastic, and very handsome with blonde hair and laughing green eyes. The combination made it hard for the sisters to refuse his request, not to mention it was their father's business and Dawnelle's invention they would be promoting. They listened to Lou's sales pitch with open minds and hearts.

After several days of struggling for the 'right' slogan and presentation of the new product, a premiere viewing of the video just completed was scheduled for presentation to the family and advertising staff on the first day of December. Excitement pervaded the air as each board member found a chair in the conference room. Since the girls had not seen the sample video, their nerves were searching for release and relief. They looked at each other, grabbed hands, then glanced at their parents sitting on either side of them. Mom didn't usually attend the board meetings. This was a special time for her. The cream she had tried seemed to be very encouraging. She felt the lines around her eyes were diminishing. Her perception was 'Jewel of Disguise' was a wonderful product, not only because her daughter had discovered it, but her own part in the testing and being an explorer. However cautious at first, she felt the new product should be on the market.

Soothing music and aesthetic scenes of the Washington coast, the mountains, and then two lovely ladies walking slowly along the shore of a quiet part of Lake Washington come into view. Their soft pastel dresses flow gently in the breeze. A shaft of sunlight streaming like silver through the tall evergreen trees surrounding the lake, interrupted by a glimpse of an eagle soaring across fleecy clouds in a rich blue sky, draws attention. Then the scene shifts to a close-up view of a contagious smile on one of the charming maidens with porcelain smooth skin, and on to the other equally attractive miss. Softly spoken words, *"Try 'Jewel of Disguise,' a new magical wrinkle free, skin cream by Collins Cosmetics"* is heard, as well as printed words with the name of the product, flowing slowly across the bottom of the screen. The picture then fades away with softly playing music as background.

"A masterpiece," Mr. Collins exclaimed. He stood up immediately, grasping Louis Markham's hand, then hugged his daughters. Everyone present expressed their delight with the commercial. Even the girls voiced their satisfaction, though utterly embarrassed from the compliments they received, exchanging them for words of praise for Mr. Markham.

Sales of the new cream soared, once the advertising video was released to major television stations. To their amazement, the girls became celebrities seemingly over night. Neither one could walk down the street without people staring at them, even when they were separate. Some folks even stopped to ask if they were the ones they'd seen in the television commercial. After agreeing, they would encourage their admirers to buy the product. Sometimes they gave their admirers a tiny sample of the new product. More commercials were produced with the twins taking part. Their lives were kept busy revolving around the business, leaving very little time for a social life. Lou Markham, and one of the men in the office where Rochelle worked, asked them to dinner and a movie once in awhile. They went when a good movie was playing. But as far as the girls were concerned, their part in their father's business took top priority.

This became a concern to their mother. Two beautiful daughters, very busy ones, and yet she felt something seemed to be lacking in their lives. They were not the exuberant girls they had been before they had left on their trip south earlier in the summer. It was obvious that they were dedicated to their work, but she felt they needed more in their lives than an occupation. They needed a social life. Of course they enjoyed being involved in their church life. So as a caring mother, her daily prayers included her concern for her daughters.

One Sunday at church, Mrs. Collins learned from a friend that a Girl Scout troop needed a leader for middle school age girls. Through the course of conversation at dinner that evening she happened to mention the need.

"Would one of you girls know of someone who might like to take on a bunch of young teen-age girls once a week and lead them in Girl Scouting?" She asked with a loving heart.

"I used to love Girl Scouts," Dawnelle said to no one in particular.

"Yeh! Do you remember all the neat things we used to make, and the time we went to the airport and actually sat in an airplane for the first time? I earnestly wanted that plane to fly off to some exotic place…like Disneyland…but we were there to learn about planes and the life of a stewardess," Rochelle laughed.

"Say. Maybe we could be co-leaders for the Girl Scout troop. We could teach them some crafts we've learned and take them camping and such," excitement began to beam in Dawnelle's eyes as she spoke.

"I don't know," Rochelle contemplated, "We've been so busy with our work. But it would be fun…for a change of pace, and sister, we need a change in our lives."

Mrs. Collins smiled to herself, not saying a word. The notion had been thrown out for contemplation. Now it was up to her daughters to make a decision suitable to their desires. It would be their choosing.

After much prayer, both Dawnelle and Rochelle decided to give the Girl Scout leadership a try.

By the end of the following week, the family room had become filled with six very animated young ladies, all talking at the same time. Seeking control, Dawnelle raised her right hand in the air, "the quiet sign" they had established, until each girl saw the sign and raised their right hand, becoming silent. Eventually each girl had a chance to share what they would like to learn and engage in for the next several weeks. With Christmas so close, making cookies and crafts as gifts for the needy would be their first project. In due time, an outing, and maybe camping in the summer time they all decided would be fun.

After their charges left, the twins were bubbling over from the enthusiasm still lingering from their first meeting. They felt as young as the girls. An expectancy of new challenges rejuvenated their emotions, bringing out the playful side of the young women that had been put on hold for some time. Mama Collins released a sigh of triumph. Her girls were "back." A sparkle of joy dispersed crowded thoughts of unhappiness she had felt for her daughters. "Thank you, Lord," she sighed under her breath.

Making cookies the following week became the first task. A couple of the girl scouts were taking home economics in school, and had been allowed to practice their imaginations at home. However, the other four girls, plus and additional new member, had no idea what to do. Reading a recipe didn't seem to take much skill, as far as the Collins twins were concerned, until they discovered the younger girls couldn't figure out what tsp., oz., or c. meant; nor how to measure one-fourth, two third, or three-fourth cups of whatever. So, a lesson in cooking came first. By the time seven batches of cookies were baked, flour and dirty dishes covered the counter tops, floor, and table. Seven spirited young ladies were all full of energy and cookies.

"But are they good enough to 'give away' cookies," one of the girls questioned.

While the culinary delights cooled, the girls colored and pasted designs on several individual boxes for gift giving. After enough sampling of their cookies, that were not as well shaped or ruined while taking off the cookie sheets, everyone was amazed at how remarkably well the cookies turned out, and tasted. So each one carefully stored their creations in the colorful boxes they had designed to be delivered the next day, Sunday afternoon after church services.

Rochelle drove the sports car with three of the girls to families they knew through the church who were having financial difficulties, and gave out their colorful boxes of goodies. Dawnelle borrowed their Mother's new hybrid, and took the other four girls to distribute their boxes of cookies to patients in a nursing home, who didn't have families visiting them for various reasons. Tears flowed from captivated eyes on to elderly cheeks just for the privilege of being remembered. Each girl smiled as they handed the gift box to an elderly patient. Each of the girls learned a valuable lesson in caring and sharing, exchanging their fun project into gifts of love. She remembered a good friend's advice: "Healing Starts When Caring Begins."

The following week turned into a windy, wild and weird, threatening snow-cloudy week. With Christmas coming right around the corner, the weather was accepted without too much complaint. The Collins family discussed maybe a white Christmas could be anticipated. Several years had gone by since the lacy flakes of winter's chill had changed the landscape into a winter land of wonder they reminisced.

The week before Christmas the twins and their scouts met in the church basement, where they created lovely fans of plastic forks, ribbons and lace as gifts for their parents. Seasonal music filled the church, as they laughed and joined in singing the favorite carols, which of course led into the young girls imploring their leaders to take them caroling. Mr. and Mrs. Collins dropped by the church to check on the activities and encouraged them by offering to have hot chocolate and doughnuts ready to eat at the Collins' home when they returned. Defeated by the onslaught of entreatment, the twins gave in, pretending to be dismayed, although they had discussed the idea between each other earlier.

A grey sky hid the stars, as they walked from one neighbor's front door to the next singing their hearts out. Smiles and thoughtful comments from the captive audiences inspired the sweet voices to sing their very best, while singing 'White Christmas.' God must have been overwhelmed, for a tiny flake and then another began to ignite a magic spark of softness, scattering slivers of white through the darkness. Above, a full moon peaked through a cloud lighting a shimmering pathway. Two leaders and seven Girl Scouts had been smiled upon. By the time the carolers arrived at the Collins' house, the streets and walkways had turned to frosted white.

CHAPTER NINE

A cold winter had truly set in. The dark green evergreens were able to hide some of the naked branches of their neighboring trees of different diversities. Melting snow left remnants of splotchy mud holes here and there.

January had come and gone. It was closing in on March. The winter had been relatively nice. The second snowfall for the season had been around for a week now, which is rather unusual for Western Washington where the winters are usually mild. Splashes of purple and golden crocus had begun to wiggle their way through the frozen soil, releasing hope that spring should be on its way. With spring comes more new growth in multi—colored flowers, trees and plants of all varieties. And, with spring comes little beams of sunshine.

Along with their work at the cosmetic company, the twins had become enthralled with their girl scout troop. Each month their troop grew. Now they have ten adventuresome girls. Scout Troop Number 456 had just helped celebrate "Thinking Day," honoring the founders, Lord and Lady Baden-Powell, of both Boy and Girl Scouts. During the short troop life, they had accomplished several fun filled activities under the leadership of the Collins twins, such as: career exploration, planning an international dinner, and making mementos to take to their adopted grandparents in the nursing home. They were anxious to try some more activities. March was "cookie sale" time, along with a car wash at the church to help earn money for the upcoming trip to Victoria, British Columbia in Canada.

The trip to Victoria was in the planning stages. Passports needed to be taken care of. However, earning some funds for their three day trip over spring break was a must. The boat fare, motel, eating, and souvenir shopping would be expensive. A project was needed besides the car wash to earn some money. They were encouraged to take baby sitting jobs, house cleaning, garage sales, and any odd jobs they could come up with. The twins asked for, and were granted, three days from their heavy work load.

"V" day had finally arrived. Bright and early, after the planning and packing of suitcases etc., twelve anxious girls and two lovely leaders were on their way via the families' SUVs, to Port Angeles to catch the ferry to Vancouver Island, B.C. The road to the ferry was a beautiful trek along the Puget Sound waters.

As the ferry aimed its bow into the Canadian waters, Victoria's classical Parliament building stood out across from the royal Empress Hotel where the troop disembarked. Hanging baskets of colorful flowers whispered their perfume in a slight breeze along the streets edging the waterfront. Busy window shops were encouraging tourists to come see the enticing gifts they were selling from the 'old country.' Whiffs of bakery scents tantalized the atmosphere, begging customers to try the tastes of yummy baked goods. Double decker tour buses offered rides to different sights. The troop elected a tour to Butchart Gardens. They found flowers blooming with accents of glorious colors, as they strolled through acres of gardens: the fantastic sunken garden...probably their favorite; gardens of roses, various spring flower delights, Japanese gardens; and a variety of trees full of blossoms. The greenhouse was their choice of place to have a luncheon among the hanging floral baskets. Of course they couldn't pass up the gift shop to find something special to take home to Mom and Dad.

When they returned to downtown Victoria, they visited the museum, amazed at the scenes depicting wild animals in their natural habitat in a forest that appeared life like. There was a ship to board, and seascapes to make one feel you were a part of the scene, a small setting of a town to visit, and much more.

Visiting Victoria was a trip to a foreign country, and yet so much like places in the States. The girls were thrilled and chattered all the way home on the ferry, enchanted and full of excitement with what they saw, the different foods they'd tried, and on and on they chimed. Even though the girls were tired, no one appeared ready to slow down. The ferry trip and the drive back to Seattle found no one sleeping.

At the next troop meeting, the girls decided they wanted to go on a camping trip. Dawnelle agreed to their idea and convinced them there were many things they needed to learn before tackling the camp out. "While we're learning we can earn badges. We can earn a First Aid badge by taking a course in First Aid and make a First Aid kit. We'll need to learn safety rules, how to set up trail markers, make camp fires, set up tents, learn how to plan meals, practice astrology by locating stars to help learn directions, and what to do if we might encounter wild animals, or get lost."

Much to do in so short a time, Dawnelle thought.

Rochelle suggested they spend the next couple months learning and practicing all those things, and then set up a camp in the Collins' backyard to try out the skills they learned before the "Big" camp out.

Between work and their scout meetings, the next few weeks were very busy and exciting. The camping trip was planned for late June. The practice camp-out went well. Each girl was filled with excitement. A campfire was made by rounding up good sized rocks laying around in the flower beds to form a circle for the fire. The girls roasted wieners and marshmallows. Fun songs were sung and many jokes were shared. Some had brought chips and dips, some brought brownies and cookies for snacks. They spent the night trying to figure out the names of the stars peeking through some clouds in the heavens. Sometime after midnight the noisy bunch fell off to sleep.

They would go to a State Park in the Cascade Mountains for the real thing. Rochelle had asked Dad to check on an appropriate campground for the Girl Scout Troop's adventure.

Finally, the girls were all ready to go. They had worked hard learning their crafts and felt confident they could tackle what adventures lie ahead. Tomorrow morning they would head out in two SUVs. The twins had traded their little red sports car in for one of the vans and borrowed their Dads SUV for the other. Mom's energy saving hybrid was left for Mom and Dad to use. Each of the twins would have six girls with their gear, the tents, food, back packs and needed supplies. June had been a rainy month, saturating the ground. But the rain hadn't dampened the enthusiasm of the troop. The girls decided they needed to know how to survive in all kinds of weather.

Traffic was busy as they left the big city of Seattle, then the traffic reduced the closer they reached the Cascade Mountains. Showers continued off and on, then turned into downpours. The young girls didn't pay much attention to the rain. As they rode along, giggling could be heard as they teased each other, singing songs, while some listened to their I-Pods or engaged in text-messaging.

After awhile, they turned off the main highway to take the road leading towards their destination Dad had chosen. Suddenly, Dawnelle quickly stepped on her brakes, when a section of a hillside slid down only a few yards ahead of their SUV, blocking both sides of the road. Rochelle's vehicle wasn't far behind. Both girls grabbed their cell phones trying to decide what they should do, suddenly another slide spread across the highway not far behind Rochelle's vehicle blocking movement both ways.

The twins knew they had to stay calm, even though they were scared to death. They were responsible for their charges and keeping them as safe as possible. The twins got out of their vehicles and grabbed each other, telling the girls to stay in the vehicles. "We must not let the girls know how dangerous our situation is. If we stay calm and in charge we'll be all right," Dawnelle spoke with worry in her voice. Both twins breathed a silent prayer.

"Okay, girls. We took training for this camping trip. I guess God decided we could handle this situation. Let's stop and think what we need to do," Rochelle told the group who had their heads sticking out the windows of their cars, eyes wide open, yet not a sound came from any of the girls.

"First, I'll call 911 to get us some help," Dawnelle said.

Unfortunately, her cell phone didn't want to cooperate. "Um," she murmured to Rochelle. "My cell doesn't work up here in the mountains, or we've run out of cells. I forgot to recharge mine before we left home." She grimaced.

Rochelle tried hers. "It doesn't work either. Although this isn't a main highway, it is a popular road. I'm sure the slides will be reported soon, and the highway department will be coming as soon as they can get their equipment here and clear away the dirt and rocks."

Serena, one of the girls, started to cry, "I'm scared. I wanna go home." Several agreed, with loud, trembling voices.

Serena was the newest girl to join their troop. The twins had learned that her parents were having a lot of problems, both financial and marital. The father had lost his job in the bad economy touching so many families. They were hoping the camping trip would be a major time of uplifting to the little girl. She was the youngest of the group, but had been very well accepted among the older girls.

With kind words and compassion, the twins settled their charges down.

Dawnelle shared a thought, "You know, we have come up here many times as we were growing up with Dad and Mom. I think I remember an old cabin not far from here just a ways off the road."

"Yes, you're right. Why don't we leave a note in our cars to explain where we are going, and use some of our new learned skills by leaving trail markers showing which direction we're going," Rochelle suggested.

"Yeh!" The younger girls yelled in unison.

"Okay. Everyone needs to grab our bedding, food, and probably should take a First Aid kit or two and head out," Dawnelle agreed with an authoritative sound in her voice.

It kept the girls minds and bodies in a diversion, while they strapped on their back packs and busily left trail markers with rocks and sticks pointing in the direction they were traveling, thus, marking their pathway along the way.

"I read in a book that the Indians used to break a branch of a tree and leave it hanging. It left a clue as to which way they would go," Donna, one of the older girls, suggested.

"Did anyone bring a compass?" Someone asked.

"I did," another girl responded.

"Now let's see, when the sun is West and the left shoulder is toward the sun, then you're facing North...but we don't have any sun," one of the girls said. They all laughed.

"Well, let's not worry about that right now. At least it's not raining. We were going towards the East when driving. Let's just make our trail signs very obvious," Rochelle smiled.

It took a while, but they soon found the old run down cabin.

"Eureka!" One of the girls yelled. "I learned that in class last week. It means, ' We found it.'" One of the older girls explained.

All of the girls jumped up and down, giving each other the high-five.

With a little effort from the twins, the door was opened and they managed their way in and found...a disaster. Broken windows, broken furniture, dirt and dust lie all over the two room cabin.

"Oh, No!"

"Ugh!"

"Yuck!"

Groans of all kinds sprang out from their charges.

"That's okay!" Rochelle tried to sound hopeful. "'There's a rose in this rubbish that with a little work will blossom and bloom...as my grandma used to say."

"Let's get busy and clean this place up. Then we'll fix us a bite to eat," Dawnelle smiled. "Find some branches from the fir trees. We'll use them for brooms. If we all pitch in, we'll have this little ol' cabin in good enough shape to spend the night, if we need to."

"Let's sing a song as we work and make it a fun time," the oldest of the girls cheerfully suggested. She started to sing a fun song. All the girls joined in.

Another one of the girls let out a curdling scream, when a field mouse ran from under the table. Spiders and insects streaked across the floor, as cob webs and dust fell from the shelves being cleaned with enthusiasm. It wasn't long until the little cabin looked...well...liveable.

"I believe I hear the sound of a creek not far away," Dawnelle soon replied. "Grab the roll of paper towels. Let's head on through the trees and find the creek so we can wash up."

"Be careful. Not too close, you might fall in," Rochelle yelled at one of the girls, when they found the casually flowing stream.

After returning from the small creek, the twins set out the picnic lunch they had prepared before leaving home, and placed it on the little table they were able to salvage. Everyone acted as if they were starved, while they scrambled for the food.

"Wait a minute," Dawnelle raised her hands. "Let's thank God for the food, for leading us to this cabin, and for our safety from the mud slides."

"And for stopping the rain." One of the girls called out. They all laughingly agreed.

All the heads were bowed, a prayer of thanksgiving was said by Rochelle, and the picnic food was quickly gobbled up.

"Okay, girls," Dawnelle quieted the ambitious group. "Let's put to use some of the things we have learned while preparing for our camping trip. I would like us to take a little hike close to the cabin and talk about some safety rules. First of all, remember we Never Leave the Group! Never go anywhere by ourselves. But, what should we do if we do get lost?"

"Stop! Be calm. Think where we are," a blond girl spoke up.

"Settle down and rest, and think what we should do," another shared.

"Leave signs to be plainly seen as to which way we are going." A girl in a green coat said.

"Blow a whistle," and one girl did blow her whistle she had dangling around her neck on a chain.

"Sing loudly," the one girl that loves to sing suggested.

"Ohh, not you with your croaky voice," the little red haired girl giggled. Everyone joined in with laughter. But it didn't stop the singer from singing.

"Use a mirror, or flashlight for signaling," said a girl taller than the rest.

"What about poisonous plants?" Rochelle asked. "Let's make sure we remember what poison ivy or poison oak looks like. I'm sure there's one or the other, or maybe both in the woods. Let's search. The first to find either one call out, but don't touch."

"How about wild animals? We talked about what to do and not do when you see one. And, those we need to avoid. Put your minds to work. Help each other and stay together," was Dawnelle's wise advice.

It was getting dark, so the troop followed their markings back to the cabin, grabbing some dry sticks to use for starting a fire in the little wooden stove big enough for the one pot they had found and cleaned down by the creek. Several large cans of chili were warmed up and served with crackers, one of the girls had brought for snacks. Another cheerfully passed around a bag of candy for dessert.

"Let's make a campfire and roast some marshmallows," Dawnelle suggested with firm approval from all.

Silly campfire songs were sung. Rochelle and Dawnelle

shared some stories they remembered from their scout days. An owl hooted in the background, causing the girls to squeeze closer together. They claimed they weren't scared, just wanted company. Yawns were heard from one girl, then another. Yawning seemed to go around.

"Time to put out the rest of the fire, which had turned to coals, and see if we can make room in the little house to sleep. The one bed isn't very good, but whoever gets there first gets the bed," Dawnelle grinned, and quickly moved out of the way of the herd trampling by.

A scramble for the door caused some jovial pushing and shoving, until two young ladies jumped in the middle of the bed. Plop! It fell to the floor, splitting in two at the middle. Everyone began to laugh, 'cause no one really got to sleep on the feather mattress. Feathers were flying all over the room, however. So everyone decided they each had a feather mattress on the floor beneath their sleeping bags. The giggles and comradery soon calmed down and everyone finally fell into an exhausted sleep.

No one admitted hearing the rustle of tree branches scraping the sides of the cabin, or a coyote howling in the background, or some crawly creature running across the roof top. It wasn't scary, just annoying. Both troop leaders commented to each other about how proud they were of the attitudes of their charges. They felt so pleased, since the circumstances and poor attitudes could have made it so much worse.

Morning came early, when the yummy smells of bacon and pancakes sizzled on the stove. Rochelle had ventured back to her SUV to find the cooking utensils and ingredients for breakfast. Good ol' boxed mixes and powdered milk and paper plates were very handy for this occasion. Everyone ate greedily, along with the chattering and teasing among the troop, about last nights sounds.

By the third night Dawnelle and Rochelle talked among themselves, getting a little concerned that no one had come to their rescue. Still, they had enough supplies to last them for a week of camping. None of the parents or their folks knew the situation they were in, since their cell phones were evidently out of commission from the mountainous territory. The girls were having fun, enjoying their stay, roaming the woods, sharing their thoughts, but not realizing they were trapped until the slides were cleared away. The twins felt very fortunate for the good comradery the scouts shared. The older girls of the troop looked out for the younger ones, especially Serena. Very little arguing and fussing was heard.

CHAPTER TEN

By the end of the week, Grant and Leslie Collins were feeling a little concerned because they had not heard from their daughters. Their girls promised to call when they got to their camp site, but the parents received no word. When they tried numerous times to call their cell phone, their messages were never acknowledged, nor proclaimed out of service.

"I know the girls are busy and having fun, but it's not like our girls to not answer our messages, Grant. I'm getting a little concerned," Mom said in a caring tone.

"I agree with you, honey. Maybe we'd better start checking," her husband spoke in accord.

After Grant started making some phone calls, he became more concerned. He learned the highway department had closed down the highway the group would have traveled on. The mountain roads had been closed because several dangerous slides had been reported. Now, TV news reporters were claiming a fire had started to spread toward the area of the campground the girls would have taken their Girl Scout troop for the camping trip…under his advice.

The phone began ringing from the parents concerning their children in the Girl Scout troop. Mrs. Collins didn't really know what to tell them, since they hadn't heard any response from the numerous phone calls they had tried to make to their daughters.

In the meantime, two young men with their helicopter were in the Northwest fighting fires. They had been in great demand this year with their helicopter and fire fighting skills they possessed. It had become a long busy business, because of droughts and lighting, causing so many dangers in California, Oregon, Washington and all the northwest forests. Because of their willingness to join other fire fighters, Lance and Lyle had become heros to many people who would have lost their homes and/or their businesses.

Lance and Lyle had been assigned to the Cascade Mountains in the Washington State fire region. While flying over the area, they spotted two vehicles on a lonely road in between two huge mud slides. They became concerned, even though they couldn't see any damage to the sports vans. They couldn't see any one around them. Maybe the people had already been rescued, but they decided to call in the report and inform dispatch that they would investigate the area to see if there was any sign of trouble.

About a mile from the vehicles, they finally located a clearing large and safe enough to land their chopper. With some difficulty in walking the terrain, they managed to work their way back to the area where they had spotted the two vans.

Lance checked one van while Lyle checked the other. They both found a note in each van telling where to find the cabin locating where a Girl Scout troop could be found. Then set forth to follow the well marked trail the troop had evidently made leading to the cabin. There was no sign of life around the building. When they knocked on the door, there was no answer. But, they opened the door and found sleeping bags and other paraphernalia. Not knowing where the troop might have gone, they decided to stay there at least for awhile and hope the people would be back soon, as they sat swatting mosquitos.

It wasn't long until they heard chattering and laughter. One of the men opened the door and startled the group of girls approaching. It was obvious they were frightened and started screaming, "Who are you? What are you doing in our cabin?"

Several of the girls started to run away to find their leaders, who were taking their time enjoying the scenery and the quietness of the woods. After hearing the girls screaming, however, the twins ran to see what was the matter. Before they got to the cabin, they yelled to the girls to run back into the woods to hide.

During the mayhem, the men were trying to explain to the girls who had reached the cabin first that they were there to help them. But the girls couldn't understand why they needed help, and kept telling them to leave.

Finally, Lance noticed one of the ladies and called out to her. "It's all right. We're here to rescue you and your girls from a fire that is getting too close."

"Rescue us? A fire! We didn't know there was a fire. We didn't notice or smell any smoke."

"It's on the other side of a ridge. You can't see it from here. Didn't you hear it on the radio?"

"We didn't bring a radio," Dawnelle said apologetically, as she put her hand over her mouth embarrassed. "Oh, dear. That's one thing I didn't even think about." Then she really looked at the man. "I think I know you, aren't you Lance...or...Lyle Taylor?"

"Yes, ma'am. I'm Lance. We've been asked to come here to the northwest to help put out fires," he grinned that charming grin at her. "I didn't think we'd ever see you again, since you left the Grand Canyon in such a hurry," Lance expressed, a solemn expression on his face.

"We left a note with our address and phone number at the ranger station stating that we had to leave because mother was in the hospital. But you never called, so we thought you didn't care." Dawnelle looked, what was it hurt or angry; probably both?

"I'm sorry. We never found your note. We were asked to help with a fire in the California mountains, and had to leave right away, after we had left you that night of Thanks-giving. Sorry we didn't get to say good-bye," Lance frowned.

"I...a...we missed you guys. We really enjoyed being with you." Dawnelle's eyes shown relief, as well as sadness.

"Where are the rest of your party?" Lyle asked. "We really need to get all of you out of here. It will take some time. How many are there, and what group are they? I'll need to inform headquarters that all is well."

"We have twelve girls, Dawnelle and me." Rochelle entered the conversation now. She looked at Lyle standing next to Lance, smiling shyly.

"Call your girls and let's get moving," Lyle encouraged, yet speaking with authority.

They could only bring their back packs and safely squeeze six girls in the chopper at a time.

He informed them.

It wasn't long until they had all reached the helicopter. Lance immediately called in the report to the authorities to let them know their situation, and that the Girl Scout Troop were in the process of being rescued. They could only bring their back packs, and safely squeeze six girls in the chopper at a time. Lyle did the piloting, while Lance stayed behind with the rest of the troop. The girls were excited about riding in the 'copter. Lyle flew them to a safe place. During the flight he had radioed ahead to a location where their parents could be waiting, anxious to see their children. He learned the fire was spreading faster because of winds. So, he dropped his passengers off, with helpers already there to assist, until their parents could arrive. Then he headed back to pick up the other girls without haste.

After all the younger girls had been dropped off at the safe place, Lyle returned after the twins and his brother. The mission was getting riskier by the minute, as the flames were now visible, and drawing closer to the victims. Yet he knew the chopper was the only way out. The three quickly boarded the helicopter, then he flew out immediately. They were all sorry they didn't have time nor room for any of the camping equipment. Their SUV's would probably be destroyed, since the vehicles had to be left behind. But those things could be replaced eventually. Both twins voiced a prayer of thanks during the trip out of danger. Every one was thankfully relieved that all of their lives were spared.

"We really need to get back to fighting the fire," Lance finally spoke with concern.

As each one expressed their thankfulness to their heros, the men told them, "It was all in a days work."

Before the men left the young women with their Scout troop and their families, Rochelle quickly wrote their address and phone number on a piece of scratch paper she found in her pocket.

"We want to see you again," both Dawnelle and Rochelle called out at the same time.

The guys both grinned, waved, and called back they would find them, as they boarded their helicopter.

CHAPTER ELEVEN

The story of the rescued Girl Scout Troop made the television news that night on several televison channels. They were all a little embarrassed when interviewed, because they really didn't know they had been in danger, but expressed their thankfulness to the TV reporters for the two heros that had rescued them.

It was several days later, late in the afternoon, when Dawnelle answered a knock on the door. When she opened it, there stood two very handsome young men with big grins on their faces. She squealed loudly, calling Rochelle to come quick. Rochelle ran to the door. She squealed just as loud, if not louder than her sister.

"Uh, may we come in?" Lance was still ginning. "We'd have been here sooner, but we had a little trouble finding where you lived."

"Oh, yes, come in," Rochelle pulled Lyle in, while Dawnelle grabbed Lance's arm.

"What's all this racket going on," Mr. Collins came to the

door, with his wife close behind. Both were grinning at the young folks.

"Daddy. Mother. These are our two heros, Lance and Lyle Taylor. The Rangers we told you about. The ones we met at the Grand Canyon, and the ones who saved us from the recent fire."

"You both are very welcome. Come in, come in," Mr. Collins grabbed one of the hands of each man, shaking both men's hands at the same time. It was easily perceived that his enthusiastic hand shake showed how grateful he was to the Rangers.

"We are just getting ready for dinner. Will you join us?" Mrs. Collins smiled at them with tears in her eyes. "You must stay so we can get to know you."

"We'd be honored, Mr. and Mrs. Collins," they both spoke the same words together.

"My, my. Another set of identical twins. How in the world will we be able to tell you a part. I've had enough trouble telling our girls apart," she laughed.

"I think we've got the differences worked out, Mama. But I'm not sure we're going to give our secret away," Rochelle giggled.

"Oh, you girls. You've always loved to tease us. I think I'm going to have to think up some way and not let you know," she said with a smile.

They all laughed.

Dinner was delicious as usual. The conversation was fun, as each one got to know each other a little better. The love that showed in the Collins family was very obvious. During the meal, the young men shared some of their background with the parents.

Their father had been a pilot for a well known airlines, and had often taken their children for trips around Arizona, teaching the sons how to fly in his own private plane. Flying just merged into their blood.

The young men had survived two tours of Iraq flying helicopters only to come home a few weeks after their last tour, when their parents had been killed in a car accident by a drunk driver. The family was devastated. But they decided to go into the helicopter business from the money they had saved, along with their part of the inheritance they had received from their parents. The business was going real well, even though they decided to move up to the northwest, when they got back from fighting the fires in California.

Lance looked at Dawnelle then, "We wanted to see if we could locate the girls. We saw some commercials on TV and couldn't believe our eyes, when we realized it was Dawnelle and Rochelle. They are so beautiful. We felt we didn't have anything to offer them, with us just starting up a new business again. So, we didn't try to look them up."

"Also, we both didn't think they had really cared about us, when they left the Grand Canyon so suddenly without any word. We were afraid we may have come on too strong," Lyle shared, while looking at Rochelle.

"Oh, we're so sorry," both girls spoke together with sorrowful eyes.

"We did leave a note with our address and phone number at the Ranger Station explaining why we had to leave so suddenly. The ranger who was sitting at the desk promised he would see that one of you got the note," Dawnelle said.

"We found you now, though. We'd like to get to know you better, if it's all right with your folks." Lance shared, while looking at both parents.

"No problem. Please know you will always be welcome in

our home," Mr. Collins replied, with a smile and nod of agreement from Mrs. Collins as well.

The parents left their visitors fairly early to work on the business books laid out in the adjoining office, and allow the two couples their privacy. The men stayed for a while longer, not wanting to leave, but both were exhausted from their fire fighting that day. Eventually they said they'd better head for home, promising they'd be back. They had an apartment several miles out of town and needed some rest. Arrangements were made to get together for dinner and a baseball game on Friday night.

The girls walked the men to the door. The guys both stopped and took the hands of each girl. "Uh, are you Rochelle?" Lyle asked with a confused grin on his face.

A giggle come forward from Dawnelle, "No."

He quickly took the hand of the other twin.

Lance took Dawnelle into his arms about the same time Lyle took Rochelle into his. Each one was in their own little world. A sweet kiss tenderly touched the lips of each partner. Bells began to ring and butterflies began to fly around in the girls stomachs. Heaven surely couldn't be any better than this.

Eventually the guys said they really needed to leave.

Friday night couldn't get there soon enough. The girls waved good bye and dreamily wandered up to their own bedrooms. Could life get any sweeter?

"Night Mom and Dad. Sweet dreams," the girls whispered to each other with smiles on their faces. They heard Mom and Dad say their goodnights, but there was no return answer.

CHAPTER TWELVE

During the week the Collins' family received a call from the highway department informing them that their SUVs had been located and in good condition, if they would like to retrieve them. The rocks and mud had been cleared. They were all thankful with the news. The girls decided to call Lance and Lyle to see if they might be able to help drive the vans back. Both men were pleased to offer their services. Early Saturday morning would be the best day for them to take some time off from their work. They would still be able to eat dinner out and hopefully attend the Mariners ball game as they had originally planned on Friday.

Friday was an invigorating day. It seemed to go by so slow, but when the guys came by to pick the girls up, it seemed to go too fast. Dinner was wonderful, and the Mariners won the ball game. So everything turned out just right.

Saturday was a nice day in Seattle. The sun was beaming through the puffy white clouds with a warmth in the air that didn't require even a sweater. Still, they decided they might need one while in the mountains. On the way the girls wanted to stop at a store to purchase some cleaning supplies and some boards to enclose the broken windows of the cabin. They had already brought along a hand saw, hammer and nails. Once they arrived at the turnoff to where the cars were located, there was no sign of the dirt and rock slides on the highway, leaving an impression as though nothing bad had even happened to the road. The vehicles had been moved to the side of the highway so other cars could pass by. After careful inspection, no damage had occurred to either SUV. They were pleased that the vans both appeared in good condition.

The drive to the cabin wasn't far, and in no time at all the girls set out to clean up the cottage and get it back into a better appearance, while the men nailed boards over the windows, and was able to put the bed back together. Except for the broken windows and being messy inside, they all decided the cabin was structurally in sound shape. The owners might even be pleased that they left it in a little more presentable condition, after twelve teenagers and two young women had been staying there for nearly a week. It didn't take the four long to clean and pack up what had been left behind. Dawnelle wrote a note with their e-mail address as well as their home phone number and address, which was left on the table thanking the owners for their use of the cabin during the emergency, and for the owners to contact them if they should so desire.

During their journey back to the vans, Dawnelle noticed a beautiful wild flower, one she didn't remember seeing before, and didn't recognize. It was something like the wild tiger lily only much larger with white petals as big as her hand and coppery stripes streaming down the sides. Not only was it even more beautiful, but had an exotic fragrance. She asked the group to stop. As they all scouted around, they found several more of the beautiful flowers in clumps of the same distinct species. Dawnelle decided to dig up several clumps of the beauties and take them home. She placed the plants with plenty of dirt in several paper towels saying, "Sometimes scientists have located a rare plant and found they were good for medicinal purposes. Maybe we can use these in our cosmetics. It would be fun to experiment with such a nostalgic flower and see if it is truly something special." She was teased, by the rest of the group, but that didn't discourage her. Biology had been one of her most exciting subjects in college. "Maybe I could come up with a nonexistent product. Who knows?" She answered their good natured teasing.

So engrossed in their new find, Dawnelle wasn't watching where she was walking when she fell over a mossy log, landing right smack dab on her face. Lance quickly went to her rescue, "Are you hurt?" His concerned expression shown fear clearly on his face.

"No. I just hope I didn't hurt these plants." She started to get up with a pouting expression on her lovely face, noticing she had landed on the prized possessions. After a brief inspection, she found they didn't look any worse for wear, yet her face was covered with green moss and dirt. With a slight chuckle, Lance pulled a clean hanky from his pocket and began to wipe off the grime from her face and brush it out of her hair, while he tried to contain a big grin spreading across his striking face. She stuck her tongue out at him. A loud roaring laugh finally came out. The other two followed with a hardy laugh.

Rochelle brought out the paper towels that were left, and the hand sanitizer she was carrying in her pocket and gave it to her sister. "I think you're going to live. Are you well enough to head for home?" She teased, still smiling at her sisters smudged face.

With three vehicles to drive now, and since each one thought they were starved, they eventually called each other with their cell phones about making plans to stop at a golden arches and grab a quick meal. After a short stop, they aimed their vehicles towards home.

As soon as they arrived home, Dawnelle set out to plant all but one of the treasured delights in their back yard in the shade under a fir tree. This would be similar to the location where she had found the little jewels in the woods. The other one she decided to take to the cosmetic company to see what the special plant had to offer.

Several days went by. Dawnelle arrived home a little later than usual from work each day. One evening a big grin was plastered all over her face, when she entered the family room. With a beam in her eyes, she proclaimed to her family she had come up with a grand discovery; a cream as soft as velvet with a mystical fragrance.

Unfortunately, the family wasn't quite as excited as Dawnelle. Disappointment clearly shown on her face, still she wasn't letting that deter her thoughts about making another cosmetic product. She really felt she had come up with something exciting. She glanced out the window into the backyard and noticed that the specimens she had planted a few days ago were bigger and looked like they were already spreading. "Look! The flowers are having babies," she exclaimed to whoever would listen.

Both girls ran outdoors to check their find. The floral display was beautiful, and appeared to be multiplying. Now they were both excited. "I believe Kathleen, my nurse in Arizona, cast an Irish spell on you, Dawnelle," her sister exclaimed.

"Well, I don't really know, Rochelle. Maybe so," Dawnelle grinned.

"I used some of the same ingredients as I had in the new

cream I made before. You know, 'the Jewel of Disguise'?" Dawnelle explained. "Only I added some oil I pressed out from our new flower, took out the skin coloring, and this is what I come up with." She took out a little jar and rubbed it on the back of Rochelle's hand and told her to smell it.

"Ohhh, it's heavenly and so soft. The fragrance is one I can't explain," then Rochelle's eyes became real dreamlike. "I love it." For an hour Rochelle wandered around the house with dreamy eyes.

"What's wrong with Rochelle?" Dad Collins grinned at his daughter. "She looks like she's in a trance. A lovely one," his white teeth shined.

"I had her rub some of the cream, I developed, on her hand," Dawnelle answered.

"Hey, rub some on your Mother's hands," he laughed.

"Okay. I'll try some," Mom Collins agreed, reaching out her hand and smiling. Pretty soon she was looking dreamy eyed and gave her husband a romantic kiss.

"Wow! Give me some of that cream!" He grabbed the jar and rubbed some on his cheek. Mr. Collins became as dreamy eyed and presented gestures of compassion to the other members of his family.

Dawnelle became thoughtful. *"What have I created? Should I carry on with the testing? It doesn't appear to be dangerous. Maybe it could be a fun cream. Hmm, maybe I could try it on Lance and Lyle?"* She grinned to herself. *"They are supposed to come for dinner tomorrow night. Ah-ha. That would be fun to try it out on them, too."* She grinned to herself.

Tomorrow couldn't come soon enough in her way of thinking. She wouldn't tell her family her plan, but she did run out to the garden and pick a few more blossoms from one of the treasured plants that was continuing the multiplying process.

While at work the following day, Dawnelle prepared some more of her new discovery and placed it in a jar. Louis Markham happened to come by the laboratory where she worked and asked how things were going. She told him just fine. Would he like to try some of the new cream she was working with. His demeanor wasn't the usual congenial attitude he usually shown.

He sort of groaned, but told her to go ahead and rub some on his wrist. Immediately his attitude changed. Another employee happened to walk by at that moment. He reached out and grabbed her in his arms and kissed her. They both looked astonished.

"Mr Markham!" The lovely lady's face was beet red.

"A-aa, I'm so sorry, ma'am. I don't know what came over me," then he reached for her again. This time the kiss was even more passionate.

Dawnelle couldn't help grinning big time now. *"What in the world is in that flower to cause such an outrageous reaction?"* She couldn't help but become bewildered. *"I wonder if it could become dangerous,"* she giggled to herself, wondering what the after effects would be. But she still couldn't wait to try it on the twins.

Finally, she interrupted the embraced couple with a little cough, "I'm sorry to bother…you two, but…maybe we'd better get back to work? I have guests coming for dinner tonight, and I have some work to finish before I leave." The two red faces mumbled something, as they both went their separate ways.

Later that evening around 6:00 p.m., the girls were helping their mother finish up the preparations for dinner, when the doorbell rang. Rochelle quickly went to the door and received their company of two very attractive young men. Every time she greets the guys they seem so special to her. After the welcome, they were escorted to the table where a dinner of roast beef and all the trimmings were being placed on the table. Conversation among the family was genuine and pleasant. Everyone seemed interested in each other. They tried not to speak all at once. The meal ended in good spirits and laughter. For dessert Dawnelle said she had something special she wanted to give each one. With that, she placed a small jar in front of each person at the table, then told everyone to please try her latest discovery, to rub just a little bit on their arms. The family looked at each other and grinned, then took and opened their jars. The Taylor men followed suit. Then Lyle wanted to know if it was edible. Dawnelle shook her head no, then asked every one, again, to rub a small amount on their wrist. It was only a few moments when the demeanor on each face changed to that dreamy—eyed look. No one can remember being at the Collins table with so much smooching going on. But tonight was the night.

After awhile Dawnelle called the 'meeting' to order, "My dear loved ones," she laughed out loud, "I'm a little bit sorry for playing a trick on you. But I wanted to see if my cream really is a 'Cream of Romance.' That is what I decided to call it. I tried it on Lou yesterday, when he looked so down in the dumps. And, Wow! He immediately changed. I think we now have a new romance blossoming at work. He had reached out and grabbed Melissa, as she was walking by and kissed her several times, after I had him rub some on his hand. I knew she has liked him ever since he first came to work at the company. He liked her, too, but was too shy to get a romance started. Now it looks like the cream has brought them together.

"What do you think? Should we go ahead and market this cream? Daddy?"

"Hmm. I'm not sure. At first it might be fun. And I'm sure we could sell it with the right kind of advertising, but would it cause any problems? What are the after effects? I don't know. I think we should really be careful. We should probably wait and experiment with it a little more. Maybe tone it down some."

"One thing I think is good about the cream, the spell doesn't last all that long and it is very energizing, as well as leaves such a nice velvety feel to the skin. Maybe if I don't use a lot of the oil from the flower it won't cause any problems." Dawnelle was thinking out loud. "And another thing, I really think it has a calming affect. I'm really tempted to use it on an angry person, or a dog, or something, or someone to help change an attitude. What do you all think?" she asked.

"I rather like that idea," Lance spoke. "You can try it on me right now!" He grinned.

"Oh, silly. You just want that romantic feeling again," she winked and scrunched up her nose and grinned.

"Yeh, I wouldn't mind trying it as an experiment" Lyle joined in.

"You guys! You don't need a love potion," Rochelle laughed.

A few days later, after Dawnelle tried different ways of using her cream, the girls decided to take a walk in their neighborhood. "Oh, oh. Do you hear a loud barking?" One of the girls said, "It really sounds rather malicious."

Rochelle decided they had better check on the situation, when they heard a child's voice screaming and running their way.

Dawnelle caught the little girl who cried out, "He's going to bite me!" Then she noticed it was Serena, their little girl scout friend.

"Okay, honey. Try to calm down."

"But I want to go home and I have to go that way," she pointed and was shaking now.

"We'll walk with you past the dog, on the other side of the street. He's fenced in so he can't hurt you," Rochelle tried to encourage the little girl. "The best thing to do is act like you aren't afraid, because the dog can sense your fear."

As Rochelle started to walk Serena towards her home, Dawnelle crossed the street where the dog was still barking, took out a little spray bottle from her jacket, and sprayed it towards the animal. She wasn't sure what would happen, but this was her chance to find out if her new formula she had revised into an oil was going to be of any help. Immediately the dog calmed down, and became as docile as a purring kitten. She was thrilled.

Both twins and the little girl were grinning now.

"We'll walk you on to your home, Serena." They of course had met her parents before as Girl Scout leaders, and as neighbors living not far down the street from their home. They decided to talk to the parents. The mother, Mary, met them at the door and noticed Serena had been upset. Rochelle explained what had happened.

Mary was so pleased that they took time to walk her home. The mother appeared to have been crying. "This has been a terrible day. John and I have decided to get a divorce. We just can't seem to get along anymore."

"I'm so sorry, Mary. Is there anything we can do for you?" Dawnelle wasn't surprised with the news, but felt badly for the dear lady.

"Just keep us in your prayers. I really don't want a divorce, but John doesn't want to go for counseling. If he would, maybe we could work out our problems."

Dawnelle thought for a minute, then decided she had to try something. "I would like to give you something. I want you to promise me you'll try it. It's a cream I've been developing at Dad's cosmetic business. She handed a little jar to Mary. "When

John comes home this evening, rub some of it on his arm and see what happens. It won't hurt to try," she smiled.

Mary took the small container of cream Dawnelle offered her, opened the lid and smelled it. "Umm, the fragrance is wonderful. Should I try it?"

Rochelle grinned, "I think it would be more pleasing to try it on your husband first. Then you could rub some on your arm."

"Well, I'll try anything to help our marriage. Thanks to you for helping Serena, and for the cream. I hope it will help."

"Please let us know how you are doing, and if the cream does anything for you," Dawnelle spoke with a smile.

"You come see us sometime. And you visit us again, Serena. Maybe it would be best for you to walk across the street from where the dog lives, so you won't disturb him when you walk by," Rochelle encouraged their small friend some more. She really was a beautiful little girl with big green eyes and light brown hair.

Dawnelle couldn't wait until they got back home. She was so excited about the calming of the dog with her spray concoction and anxious to tell her father. Hopefully she may have really created something that would be useful…from a beautiful flower yet!

Towards the end of the next week there was a knock on the door. Mrs. Collins answered the sound of knocking. Mary was standing on the other side with a big grin on her face. "Would one of the twins be home?" She asked.

"Dawnelle's up in her room. Come in and I'll call her."

When Dawnelle arrived in the living room, she welcomed the guest, "What can I do for you, Mary?" She smiled.

"Oh, Dawnelle. You've already helped me out so much. I can never thank you enough. When John came home the night you walked Serena back to the house, I took him aside and showed him the jar of cream. I explained where it came from, but not what it did because I didn't know. Then I asked him if I could rub some of it on his arm. He wasn't very excited about it, but he let me. You won't believe this, but after rubbing his arm with the cream, and maybe five minutes later, probably less, he took me in his arms and kissed me like he used to when we were dating. I was dumfounded, but enjoyed every minute of it," she was grinning now.

"What did you put in that cream? I want to buy a five gallon jar of it!" She laughed. "Our lives have changed over night. John actually says he loves me and wants to take me out to dinner tonight, even go to Blake Island to the Salmon dinner and Indian production. We haven't done that in ages and ages. Now I need to find a babysitter for Serena."

"Bring Serena over here tonight. I'd love to take care of her," Mrs. Collins expressed her offer with a lovely smile. She had known about Mary and John's problems through the prayer list at church, and was very willing to help in any way she could.

"I am thrilled my experiment went so well." Dawnelle told her. "It's a new substance I have recently developed in father's cosmetic company. I've tried it on my family. You're the first outside of the family, Mary." Dawnelle was so encouraged with the product now. She really wanted to do something to help people. Maybe, just maybe this would be her chance. She couldn't wait to tell her father of this latest experience, hoping he wouldn't be late getting home from work tonight. "Oh, he has a meeting tonight! Shucks!"

CHAPTER THIRTEEN

It has been a while since the Girl Scout troop had gotten together. The parents had felt it would be wise to take the summer off, since so many of the girls' families had plans to travel or do other things for the rest of the summer months. It was fine with the twins, since they were extra busy with their jobs, and spending as much time as possible with their new loves.

Rochelle felt they should get the girls together for passing out their badges they had earned in preparation for the camping trip earlier in the summer, as well as the other projects they had completed. The church allowed them to use the fellowship hall for their meeting, since most of them were either members or attended the church Sunday School classes.

The girls were excited about receiving their badges.

The attendance was great. The twins had decorated the fellowship hall with as many Girl Scout paraphernalia as they good gather. All the parents had come, along with many friends who wanted to support the girls. Each girl who wanted to, gave a little speech about the things they had accomplished during the year. One told about their trip to Victoria, B.C. One told about their rescue from the fire. Another girl told how much they had enjoyed all the things they had learned. Many had shared with their friends, and were excited about joining the group, and looking forward to the new year in Girl Scouts. All of the girls received badges to sew on their scarves, and felt so pleased with their accomplishments.

The new product Dawnelle had created appeared to be close to acceptance from the Collins' Board members. There were some who were cautious about producing new formulas. But she felt that wasn't unpleasant. She wanted the product to be something beneficial and worthwhile. Also, the new product might help medical practices: like people with mental problems, depression, or even Alzheimer patients. Dawnelle was thinking the spray type could work something like mace. Women could carry the spray in their purses for safety reasons. She really did want to create something useful.

One evening following a delicious dinner prepared by Mrs. C, (the nickname the guys had given her), the Collins' family and the Taylor twins gathered in the family room. Mrs. C began playing the piano of favorite old songs from the 50's and 60's. It wasn't long until the girls joined her around the piano with sweet voices in song. After a short time the father took part. The girls motioned for the two guys to join them. At first they shook their heads no, then soon the room was filled with a touch of singing delight. The girls sang soprano and alto, Dad was the bass, Lance the tenor, and Lyle the baritone.

Presently, Mrs. C stopped her beautiful playing just to listen to the quintet as they continued sharing their musical tones. The season of singing filled her heart with a sunshine of God's love. How tranquil life can be with music enriching the soul. Many people are drawn closer to God through the magnetic sound of music, she had felt it herself.

"How about singing some spiritual songs? Rochelle suggested.

"Say, maybe we could do a special for church some day. That would be fun," Mrs. C thought out loud.

"Would you guys come to church with us some Sunday morning?" Dawnelle glanced at the young men with a hopeful smile on her face.

"Hmm. We haven't been in church for quite a while. What do you say, Lyle" Lance looked at his brother with a questioning grin.

"Well, the church building might collapse, if we attended. But, sure, why not. Our parents might look down from Heaven and smile," Lyle nodded his head. "We used to sing in the choir many moons ago. It would be good to attend church at least once in a while."

"Okay. That settles it," Lance agreed, always wanting to get on the "good side" of the girls' parents.

The young women had never invited them to church before. They weren't sure if their companions would attend. Maybe this will be a good start. Their faith was very important to them, and before they really wanted to get really serious about Lance and Lyle, this would be an imperative decision for a closer relationship.

Mrs. C began playing "How Great Thou Art." It wasn't long till the rest of the group started singing along. The guys had to look over her shoulder to remember the words again. The inspirational song with all the harmony filled the room. Other beautiful hymns filled the room for about an hour.

Before long Mrs. C looked at the clock. "Oh, my! It's almost eleven o'clock. We'd better start ending this marvelous concert. Let me talk to our Minister of Music tomorrow and schedule a time when we can audition for him. I'm sure he will be interested in hearing our quintet."

They all agreed on a time to practice together, and to decide what song they would sing at the audition. The week-end would be the best time for practice for all concerned, because of their responsibilities.

The good-byes for the evening were always special. The parents went on to their room, while the girls gave the guys hugs and kisses. Lance and Lyle were going to be busy the next several days with tours for sightseers of the Pacific Coast area. A Japanese tourist group had hired them for three days of sight-seeing on the helicopter.

Mrs. C had promised to let them know about the Music Minister's answer on the following week-end. Saturday was the next time they could get together...for a great meal at the Collins' home.

The week-end rolled around fairly fast. The Board members still hadn't made a decision as to whether to produce Dawnelle's new product, but things appeared to be working out to a desirable conclusion for the company.

The church Minister of Music, Mr. Meyers, was definitely optimistic about listening to the quintet. He and the Collins' family had been good friends for several years, and he knew the musical talents the Collins' family possessed. Saturday afternoon would be a good time for the rehearsal for everyone.

Saturday has come and time to practice their harmony together. Time was swiftly passing, the quintet and Mrs. C had practiced several songs. "The King Is Coming," was their choice of music to be presented to the church, a favorite of the congregation. They took time to practice the lovely, inspiring song a couple more times before presenting their musical talents to Mr. Meyers. The guys were a little nervous about meeting the

Minister of Music, but the Collins' family felt pretty confident about their endeavor. They had been privileged to sing specials at church many times through the years, along with singing in the choir. Mrs. Collins was honored to fill in for the regular pianist, when she was sick or away. So it was not stressful for the Collins' family to be singing or taking a part in the musical programs at church.

The practice went splendidly. Mr. Meyers was thrilled with their choice of music, as well as their performance. He invited them to sing the special during next Sunday's worship service. Everyone felt very pleased. The guys felt relieved, and yet a little apprehensive. They weren't real confident that their contribution to the quintet was really needed, but Mr.Meyers, as well as the family assured them that they made a wonderful contribution.

After a busy week for the guys and the Collins' family, the following Sunday had arrived. Everyone was a little nervous, but Mr. Meyers had given the Collins' family and their friends an outstanding debut. Mrs. C played the introduction to their song. The congregation was awed by their presentation. The pastor said surely God was blessed by this new group's talent, before he began his sermon. He stressed how important it is to use the gifts God had blessed one with, whether it be in music, teaching, medical field, construction, etc. God has given everyone a gift, and He expects us to use them.

At the end of the service, people crowded around the Collins' family, Lance, and Lyle, wanting to shake their hands and express their gratitude for their contribution to the service. A friend of Mrs. Collins came to her and asked if the group could sing at a church function in a couple weeks. One of the Adult Sunday School classes was having a special birthday party for all who had birthdays that month, and she thought it would be an added attraction for the class to have the Collins' group bring special music. They could sing fun songs as well as Christian songs. Their meal would be provided as "pay."

Mrs. C motioned to the rest of the group to seek their opinion. Since it was a couple Friday evenings from the date set, it sounded fine. So they all agreed they would be happy to bring the musical entertainment for that evening.

On the way home everyone felt blessed that their musical talents went over so well. Some times they all talked at once. The guys were especially pleased, since they had never thought about "singing for their supper," so to speak.

This was just a start for the group. Other people in the congregation had asked them to bring their musical skills to other functions of the church. It wasn't long until other churches in the area had heard about "the group." Even the local radio/television manager wanted an audience with the group. So, they decided they needed to come up with a name for their quintet.

Many names were suggested among the group. They didn't realize how difficult and important it was to determine a name for a five person singing group…the appropriate name. Finally, they all agreed on "Easy Listening Five + One" for the quintet name. That way they could sing pop hits or Christian songs, plus they wanted to include Mrs. C as pianist in their introductions, although she didn't think it was necessary.

CHAPTER FOURTEEN

How quickly life can change. Some little spark; a little recognition; being thankful when you can use the gifts God has given you, and realize you can bloom wherever you are planted. Mr. Collins has always stressed, "anything worth doing is worth doing well." Life can get stagnant if we just live the routine. Choose to live each day with fresh enthusiasm. Make the best of everything with your whole heart, and remember to do it with Him, for God is the one who can give you the truest glory.

Dawnelle's new product had passed with high acclaim from the Board Members of the Collins' Cosmetic Company. Each one of the board members gradually had tried the product and found it not only fun, but they believed they should go with the idea of promoting and selling it to pharmaceutical companies. They would stress their sales pitch to medical fields to try it on depressed patients, as well as Alzheimer patients.

They must seek for more of the plant Dawnelle had been growing in their backyard. They must find a nursery or farmer who would be willing to grow the plants for sale to the Collins' Company. They had some good prospects.

The Taylor twins were keeping busy with their helicopter business. Working their business and keeping up with the engagements, for the new career in song was slowly becoming a problem. For them it gave more time with the girls, but scheduling their times for rehearsals and growing a business became a challenge.

One late evening at the Collins' home, after rehearsing for their next engagement at the Puyallup Fair coming up in September, the guys suggested maybe they should let Mr. C and the girls sing as a trio one of the nights they were scheduled to perform.

Rochelle was upset with the guys somewhat, "We've got a contract with the manager in charge of the music at the fair. He wants us all to sing. Part of the reason he hired us is because we're two sets of identical twins, and that is what he's based a lot of his advertising on. We're rather unique, and he especially likes that about our group, as well as being very good in what we do, he says. Not only the younger people come to hear our concerts, but also the older generation enjoys hearing our music that they enjoyed when they were young. He even says we've become a sensation," Rochelle smiled.

"That's all well and good, Rochelle," Lyle spoke, "Still you've got to remember that Lance and I have a tourist business to manage. It's new, and so far it is doing well. Yet it takes a lot of time to keep up the maintenance on the 'copters (they had purchased another helicopter so they could schedule both of them to fly), as well as schedule job situations around your singing group."

"'Your' singing group!" Dawnelle joined in the conversation a little heated. "It's yours, too. We can't do it without you two.

We've all been swamped in our work and our singing. Don't you guys want to sing with us anymore? Don't you enjoy it?" She couldn't hide her disappointment with the situation they were discussing.

"Hey! We're not quitting," Lance explained. "We just need to make some adjustments in our scheduling of our work and the concerts," Lance tried to smooth over the discussion.

"I guess we never realized what a success we would become when we started this group," Mrs. C smiled. "However, we don't want to cause any of us problems. Why don't we seek a little rest now. I feel we do need to fulfill this contract, which all of us agreed to, for the Puyallup Fair. I do believe we need to show our integrity in any thing we sign. We should be people of excellence in whatever we do; go the extra mile and do it right. In the future though, we must think ahead. Before we accept any engagements, we must be sure we check each ones schedules better. We need to always check with each other and agree before accepting a performance. This should be our responsibility for a smooth endeavor."

Mr. C spoke up, "I certainly agree with my wife. Let's close this discussion with a word of prayer," as he held out his hands, each joined in the circle of prayer for guidance.

The Taylor men were ready to leave right after the prayer, after giving each girl a kiss, a hug, and a smile. The girls seemed disappointed that they didn't stay longer.

Mrs. C said, "Give them and their business loving time. I'm sure your Taylor men find all of this new: the singing, rehearsing, going to church regularly, and their new travel business here in Washington. If they are meant to be for you, things will work out."

"Thank you Mom, Dad. You're the best." Both Rochelle and

Dawnelle gave their parents a kiss on the cheek and a hug, then trudged up to bed.

It was a week later in the early evening when Mr. C heard a knock, and opened the front door of their home. "Hi fellows. Come on in. Good to see you."

"Are the girls at home?" Lance asked with a grin on his face.

"They're probably up in their rooms. Come on in and I'll give them a call on the intercom," Mr. C motioned for them to enter the living room.

Both girls hurried down the stairs with smiles on their lips, still dressed in their work clothes.

"Hi guys. We've missed you. Been busy, huh?" Rochelle's face lit up with pleasure.

Lyle took Dawnelle's hand and kissed it.

"Heh, aren't you Lyle?" Dawnelle grinned.

"Oops! Sorry. Got the wrong girl, eh," his face turned red.

"Yeh, Lyle. We've got to do something about this look alike stuff." Lance entered the conversation. "This will be our job tonight. Let's really take some time to figure a way to tell each other apart."

"Okay. Let's see." Dawnelle studied Lance's face very intently. Then she stared at Lyle's. "Aha! Lance has a scar over his left eye in his eyebrow."

"I remember how that happened. Lyle and I were wrestling in the house one day and I fell and bumped my head on the coffee table. I bled all over the living room. My mother was more worried about the carpet getting stained than she was my poor head," he made a sad face.

"Oh, you poor baby," Dawnelle kissed his scarred eyebrow. "Does that make you feel better? But I will always make sure I look for that scar before I kiss one of you guys."

He just grinned that special grin.

"Okay. That will do for us guys. But what can we do about you ladies?" Lyle still wanted to be sure he kissed the right one. "Let's see. Rochelle must have a scar from her accident in Arizona," Lyle touched her face very gently, lifting her hair. "Aha, here's a scar right here, just under her bangs. I'll bet that's why you wear your hair this way to hide it."

She smiled demurely and wrinkled her nose. "I keep hoping it will go away, but maybe it is a good thing after all."

"Great! Now that's settled. Let me have a kiss," Lyle grabbed Rochelle and swung her around in a circle playing the Romeo, drooping her down in his arms. All of a sudden they fell flat on the carpet, causing laughter from everyone present.

"That's all well and good, but I think maybe it would be a better idea to have a color scheme too. Rochelle's favorite colors are blue and lavender, my favorite colors are green and pink." Dawnelle suggested.

"Hmm. That might work, except my favorite color is blue and Lyle's favorite is green," Lance grinned at Dawnelle.

"Oh, you men are hopeless," she laughed. "Anyway, I imagine you guys have been busy this past week. Whatcha been doing?" Rochelle asked.

"Yeh. Had some much needed maintenance on the 'copters to fulfill, and a couple tours to do. But we're in good shape again."

"What have you two been up to?" Lance looked at Dawnelle's lovely face with a sparkle in his eyes.

"Oh, just the same 'ol, same 'ol." Then she told them about the company accepting her newest product, and how pleased everything was going.

The guys both congratulated the family at the good news.

"Well, we have some news for you. You folks aren't the only ones who have admirers out there. We had some people recognize us as part of the "Easy Listening Five + One" and offered our quintet plus pianist a free cruise with a very popular cruise line, if we would be a part of their evening performances. It would be a week long trip on the Carribean. We would sing every other night. Our rooms and meals would be included, with a pleasing amount of pay." Lance watched the faces of the Collins' family as he described the offer.

"Wow!" Mr. C grinned his exclamation. "Leslie and I have always wanted to take a cruise. But we have been so busy with our business, we just never have taken the time."

"Oh, Grant. That would be so exciting." Mrs. C was grinning from ear to ear.

Both girls couldn't keep their squeals silent any longer. They were dancing around the room, grabbing their guys and hugging them.

"Now wait a minute," Lyle tried to calm them down. "Remember, we need to take a vote on whether we accept this job or not," his eyes were beaming with pleasure. "And we need to check our schedules to see if the middle of October will be acceptable for this new job proposition. Also, we all need to have passports."

"If you fellows agree with the date, we'll work it out at the Collins Cosmetic Company for Mrs. C, the girls and I.. As Owner/CEO of the company, I believe we can make a deal." Mr. C gave his approval with a grin. The whole family was more than pleased with this opportunity. "We need to secure our passports immediately. I know they take time to process. Also, remember, we have the Puyallup Fair performance coming up real soon. We need to concentrate on it, and maybe it will be helpful in planning our cruise performances as well. What pleases, or displeases the audience there, may help decide what to sing or make changes for the better for the cruise."

The Puyallup Fair was always a Number One for excitement in the Pacific Northwest. It advertised as being the biggest and best in Western Washington State. Nearly every year the Collins' family joined the thousands of spectators attending the enjoyable event. Now it was their turn to be able to participate three of the nights of the entertainment being held each night, including the opening date.

Having coordinating costumes for the big event were decided on. The three ladies had three dresses made to match, which they had designed themselves in the latest styles. The men decided on dark slacks, white shirts, and ties made from the same material as the ladies dresses.

The "Easy Listening Five + One" opened the entertainment at the fair by singing the popular hits of the day, which led into many fun loving songs of yesteryear. They always sang a few patriotic songs. The audience gave them their wildest applause. Mrs. C was thrilled when she noticed there were some teary eyes in the audience, when they closed each performance with a popular Christian song.

The two weeks of the fair went by very quickly. But not until they all had a chance to visit the attractions. Riding the roller coaster was full of screams by the twins, grabbing onto their partners, when their stomachs felt the car should stay on top, while clinging to their guys as it makes that fast decent down. Then slowly the coaster takes its time to climb up another hill, only to swerve and plunge down even faster. The Ferris wheel started out fine, until the guys began to rock the seats just to hear their ladies share some more shrilling sounds. However, the ever popular merry-go-round seemed to be so gentle after the former rides. But their hearts just couldn't miss most of the fun rides, where the ladies could scream the loudest and the guys could rock the hardest, so the girls could grab onto their arms in fear. Of course each man had to keep trying, until they won a stuffed animal for their sweet heart, including the father who won a huge Teddy bear for his dear wife.

The ever popular Scones, cotton candy, hamburgers and hot dogs could not be missed by the hungry tummies. Warm weather charmed most of the days. Viewing the art exhibits, crafts, landscaping, favorite hobbies, the latest gadgets, new cars, the barns corralling the horses and other animals brought by the 4-H clubs to hopefully win first prize for their favorite "best friends" were always fun to see.

When the Puyallup Fair was over, tired bodies felt encouraged that their musical tones were accepted so readily. Now, after some time of catching up on their personal jobs, especially the guys, the next big event to center their thoughts on was the upcoming cruise just a few weeks away. They knew they needed to add some more songs to their repertoire. Finding the time for rehearsals was the hardest, but very necessary for a challenging and successful performance.

CHAPTER FIFTEEN

What a thrill life can be when everything seems to be going great. The Taylor's Helicopter business was busy. They were in the process of searching for a much needed bookkeeper, secretary, and mechanic to help in running the business. Just an insignificant help for the sluggish economy to the area, but a necessary help for the Taylors.

The Collins Cosmetic Company has really leaped forward with the two new products Dawnelle had introduced. Both products were in great demand with high expectations, giving the distinguished reputation of the Collins Cosmetic Company an even higher regard. The newspaper and television commercials were still being shown, and new ones being created.

The singing group had trimmed some of their concerts back to once a month. The demand, however, was still visible and exciting.

Talk about exciting! Just a few more days and the cruise to the Carribean would be taking place. Everyone just knew they had to buy some new clothes, freshen up their sun tans, and lose a pound or two so they could eat anything and everything, since they had heard about the fabulous food available on board ship. Schedules needed to be met in their work places.

The Taylor twins had secured a very sweet, older lady in her fifties, that was willing to take on, not only the bookkeeping job but act as secretary for a while, until the business grew more established. She was a widow of two years. Two of her three children were married, and the third was serving our country in Afghanistan. After her husband's untimely death from a heart attack, loneliness quickly crept into her life. Her two daughters had married military men and were stationed in different parts of the country. Both of her daughters wanted her to move in with them. As much as she loved her girls, she didn't want to be a burden on them, but needed to have something worthwhile to do. After checking the newspaper employment adds for several months, all of a sudden the Taylor's add for a secretary and a bookkeeper seemed to blaze across the page as if just for her. Both of these jobs, she felt, were obvious for her to try for, as she had been a secretary and treasurer many years before and during her early marriage. Knowing very little about airplanes of any kind, she didn't get her hopes up, but still decided to try for both positions with the helicopter company. Her husband had worked for the Boeing company for many years in supervision, therefore she had heard a lot about planes, but that was the extent of her knowledge of them.

When the guys interviewed her, it was late in the day. Several people had come to apply for the job. But for some reason, the men just weren't pleased with their interviews. Almost ready to give up for the day, Mrs. Marina Arnold was their last hope. She had sat in the waiting room for several hours and looked tired, but well groomed and rather attractive for a mature woman.

When she answered their questions during the interview, she seemed to appeal to both of the men. Probably because she was the motherly type, was willing to learn the business, friendly, and enjoyed working with people. Lyle called her the next day and told her if she still wanted the job, it was hers. Her answer was a pleasant yes.

Earlier in the week a mechanic from the Boeing Company, who had lost his job because of company cutbacks, was hired to take care of their helicopters, and found to be a treasure. His name is Joe Torrey. Just watching his tall frame look over the big machines, they could tell he loved these aircrafts. He had been one of the few mechanics who worked on Flight test's helicopter at the Boeing Company. The guys felt very secure in leaving the business for a week with Mrs. Arnold and Joe Torrey, while they were off cruising the Carribean in less than a couple of weeks.

The men introduced Mrs. Arnold to Mr. Torrey the following Monday morning, when she arrived to begin her new employment. Lyle went over the books with Mrs. Arnold. Although different from what she had done before, she caught on to the computer program quite easily and seemed pleased with her new job. She felt comfortable answering the phone, and scheduling appointments for next weeks customers' sight seeing travels.

Joe was checking on the helicopters under Lance's supervision, when he noticed an essential part appeared to be missing in a strategic location on one of the helicopters. Lance showed him where all the parts were located in the service department in the building, and left him to seek out what he needed. Joe found the part he needed and replaced the missing part. This gave reassurance to the Taylor men. Both twins were very pleased with their two new employees.

The girls and their mother were spending as much time as they could after work for shopping. They just had to have new swim suits, and special outfits to wear aboard ship. They found a couple outfits alike for each woman to wear with the singing group. Then they took pleasure in finding matching ties and colorful shirts that would compliment their outfits for the three men to wear, and hoped the men would approve of them. Anything would be fine, if they didn't have to do the shopping, they all agreed.

Somehow all six of them found time to select the songs and rehearse for the concerts they were to perform aboard ship. Having the added help of the new employees for their helicopter business, definitely freed time for the Taylor men to be available for the needed rehearsals. The two girls shared with each other how much more relaxed and fun the guys were to be with. A lot less stress with the newly hired workers was quite apparent.

The Big day had arrived.

The Taylor twins met the Collins' family at the airport bright and early on Friday morning. A hotel near the Fort Lauderdale airport had been secured in advance. They were to be at the ship in Fort Lauderdale by 1:00 pm on Saturday, which was to leave for the Carribean at 4:00 pm. Excitement was not only felt by the two young couples, but Grant and Leslie Collins were just as exuberant. It had been a long time since they had taken a vacation, and they were thoroughly looking forward to this new experience of a cruise.

Mrs. C had been warned about sea sickness by some of her friends, so she had taken one of the sea sick pills just in case, with a bottle of more of the medicine to be easily found in her purse. She looked stylish and lovely in her new lavender pants outfit. She had her hair styled in an easy fashion, so her hair wouldn't be a problem while on board, or visiting stops for shore excursions along the way.

Mr. C appeared very charming in his leisure clothes his wife had picked out for him. He wasn't sure if he liked the lavender shirt, that could be worn outside of his pants, to match his wife's outfit. Suit and tie was the natural wear for his liking. But, he went along with the choice she had talked him into wearing.

The twin girls were extraordinary in their choice of outfits. Dawnelle wore a sun dress with the major colors of green, and Rochelle chose a similar dress with major colors of blue. They didn't want 'their' guys getting mixed up as to which twin was which.

After having help finding their designated rooms, all three rooms on the same deck and close to each other, time was spent hurriedly unpacking their suitcases in a nice sized closet with a few drawers to share. There were twin beds for the younger ones and a king size bed for the parents in their large suite. All three rooms had balconies with comfortable seating to enjoy the memorable ocean views. Each had a fruit bowl, appearing delicious, sitting on a table in between elegant chairs. The bathrooms were small, but included all the amenities they would probably need. Everyone was filled with excitement and wonder, anxious to explore the ship and enjoy this wonderful fantasy.

The huge, luxurious vessel gradually sailed out of the harbor with a loud blow of the horn and lots of people waving and shouting to have a good time, probably wishing they could be joining their friends and /or families heading out to sea. The weather was gorgeous with blue skies, a few puffy clouds, and a slight breeze flowing through the atmosphere.

They were told they would be the opening program for the night. They heard over the intercom system that a buffet had been set up in one of the dining areas. So they all met together and decided they had better grab a bite to eat, explore the beautiful ship a few minutes before changing their clothes and preparing for their concert in just a little while.

The buffet appeared very tempting with all kinds of goodies to treat the taste buds. Still, they all agreed they'd better not eat too heavy before they would sing. Maybe later, after the performance, they would enjoy some more of the scrumptious delights from the all night buffet.

They found the luxury ship full of wonderful things to do. There were several theaters for programs; several dining areas, an art gallery for an auction to take place several different days of the voyage; a beautiful open staircase with a huge floral chandelier hanging from the roof of the lovely ship, and an area with a piano and small place for dancing. Close by were various varieties of shops on several different levels; lovely comfortable lounges just for relaxation; and even a casino for those who enjoyed gambling.

It was extraordinary, their concert went very well. The audience was ready for some fun, and they gave it to them. Mr. C accepted the part of master of ceremonies, introducing each of his group. Their harmonies were well rehearsed and brought attentions alive, many times encouraging their listeners to join in on the choruses. The Taylor twins shared some jokes, teasing each other, sometimes including teasing the girls, bringing on the laughter. As always, they ended their concert with a couple patriotic songs and a Christian hymn. The audience even gave them a standing ovation, thrilling each of the "Easy Listening Quintet + One."

Nassau of the Bahamas was the first stopover for the cruise. It was a lovely island with swaying palm trees and an excellent place for shopping, and watching the children dive for money, as they waited patiently for the tourists to throw coins from the beaches. A limousine drove up along the curve. The driver got out and asked if they would like to see the island from the luxurious car. A squeal came out of the girls saying, "Yes. They had never ridden in a limo before." So all six of them piled in to take a tour of the island.

The following stop was San Juan, Puerto Rico where they walked down the cobblestone streets of Old San Juan, visiting the Gran Hotel El Convento…"the hotel with a soul." They learned the grand building had been a convent for the Nuns of Puerto Rico many ages ago. Now, it was a lovely hotel for tourists, where in the evenings Flamingo Dancers were to put on a show. They walked on by, the guys sorry they couldn't attend the evening show. At a distance, they found the lovely Governor's Mansion, and on further they discovered a statue of Christopher Columbus. They visited El Morrow Fort, Castillo de San Cristobal, a unit of San Juan National Historic site overlooking the brilliant blue waters of the Carribean. It was in Puerto Rico where a little girl wanted her picture taken with Dawnelle and Rochelle, because she said they were so pretty. There was still enough time to take a short tour of the Rain Forest of Puerto Rico.

The cruise went on to St. Thomas of the Virgin Islands. The ship rested at Charlotte Amalie, a beautiful town where fabulous homes could be seen built along the rocky hillsides. It was on St. Thomas where they visited Coral World. They watched divers feeding all kinds of schools of fish of many sizes, shapes and colors. A small post office was found, where they mailed post cards "under the sea" to friends and family back home. Coral World claims "the only underwater aquarium in the Western Hemisphere."

It was a stormy, tropical day when the ship pulled into port at Christiansted, St. Croix. Warnings were up everywhere for a possible hurricane. Everyone was relieved when the dangerous eye of the storm turned a different course, away from the island, letting everyone know the winds, although threatening, could have been worse. Because of the storm, the ship stayed an extra day, thrilling the passengers of the cruise, to be able to sight see and visit downtown with old and new scenes of Christiansted. They visited President Hamilton's home, an old sugar cane mill, and were thrilled while watching the "crab races" and, of course, feeding the birds.

CHAPTER SIXTEEN

The cruise was obviously a very enjoyable experience for those who were devoting their time for relaxation on board ship. People were friendly, and seemed to be looking for fun. Every where the guys were on board ship, bunches of young, and older women, crowded around them wanting their autographs. The only problem the girls found to be somewhat annoying was...a man seemed to be everywhere they went, at a distance. He was young. He was rather handsome, always nicely dressed, and had a nice haircut. However, a smile was never on his lips. He didn't ever say anything to them. But, his eyes were penetrating, so intense, leaving them with a feeling of danger. Was he stalking them? They really didn't know whether to say something to their family, or not. They decided not to, for now. It may be nothing at all. After all, they were here to have fun and enjoy themselves, when they weren't working. If you can call singing their hearts out, working.

Towards the end of the cruise, on one of the stopovers, Grant wanted to find a special artifact to buy for their home, while the ladies decided to brows around a ladies dress shop. The Taylor guys decided to check out one of the many jewelry stores.

While at the jewelry store, Lance and Lyle discovered a unique necklace. It was a rugged cross created from petrified wood, with a beautiful golden crown hanging from the main post. The rugged cross bore the scars, suggesting where the hands and feet of our Lord Jesus would have been nailed. In the middle of the crown was an oval shaped diamond with a mass of all sorts of lovely gems circling the crown. Lance found one that had mainly emeralds encircling the diamond and through out the crown. Lyle was pleased to find one with many sapphires. They both decided the crosses were the perfect gifts for their sweethearts.

After the shopping spree, they all found a superb restaurant where they tried some of the local selection of foods. Each tried something different…even off each other's plate. On the way back to the cruise liner, they saw a woman feeding some of the birds. All of a sudden, one of the pigeons landed on Rochelle's shoulder. She was so startled, she let out a light shrill, then laughter. Pretty soon, each one had feathery friends landing on their arms and shoulders, begging for some small parcel of food. The girls soon "apologized" to their newest friends, since they didn't have anything to feed them, and shooed them away as they walked on back toward the ship.

Time was quickly passing, so they hurried back to the cruise liner, where they changed into their outfits for the program that evening. They had a little time to gather together for a quick run through some songs they weren't sure about, before the show was to begin.

The guys presented them with the gifts they had discovered. When the girls opened up the small packages given to them, tears came to both girls eyes.

"What a beautiful gift," they both proclaimed at the same time.

"It is so awesome," Dawnelle spoke.

"Thank you so much," Rochelle hugged Lyle. "The cross even has a diamond and sapphire jewels on the crown."

"And mine has emeralds. You guys are so very thoughtful," Dawnelle kissed Lance on the cheek.

"Is that all I get," Lance teased.

Then both girls grabbed their guys and really gave them a thankful kiss. The parents stood by, smiling at the scene taking place.

"Well, put them on and lets get the show on the road," laughed Mr. C.

The evening was a big hit. The assemblage was the largest of the week, and everyone seemed to really enjoy the groups choice of songs and times of teasing. No one wanted to leave the auditorium. They kept giving them a royal encore, with whistling and clapping. Mother C started playing a favorite hymn to sing, which finally closed the evening concert.

The following evening was the last performance of the Quintet. Everyone felt just a little bit of sorrow to be ending their journey on board ship. They wore their best outfits, practiced the songs they had chosen to sing, and decided to leave a little bit early to make sure everything was in place for the performance.

As they started down the stairs, Dawnelle realized she had forgotten to wear the beautiful cross necklace Lance had given her. She told her family she wanted to go back to the room to get it, but assured them she would be right back. When she reached the bottom of the stairs, someone grabbed her arm, startling her.

"Hey! Let go of me. You're hurting my arm," Dawnelle cried out in pain.

"Calm down. I won't hurt you" the young man gave her a pointed glare.

Then she realized it was the stalker. Fear overtakes her being. "Why do you keep following my sister and me?" She questioned the man.

He didn't say a thing, just pulled her along with him, while she struggled, trying to get away. They entered a stateroom. He tossed her toward the bed, but she missed the bed and fell down on the floor. With strong hands, he grabbed her again. "Don't make a sound or I will hurt you," he warned.

"Please, don't touch me. Just tell me what you want." Dawnelle whispered. Her fear was very obvious.

"You know what I want. You and your sister look so much alike, I don't care which one I take."

Tears started to well up in her eyes and flow down her cheeks. All she could think of is to ask God for His protection. A verse comes to mind, "Resist the devil and he will flee from you. Draw near to God and He will draw near to you." (James 4:7-8)

"Look, I'm a Christian. I cannot do what you are thinking," Dawnelle felt a slight more at peace now.

"Huh. You're one of those. I should have known. A goody-two—shoes. Just shut up and I won't hurt you."

"No. I won't be a part of this. My family is expecting me any minute. They'll come looking for me," Dawnelle told him with a stubborn look on her face, shaking her head.

"You know, God created you just as much as He created me. You need to ask Him for forgiveness and change your way of thinking. You're a nice looking man. I'm sure you could have any woman you wanted. But, you need to go about it in a different way."

"Now you're going to preach to me, eh?" He said sneering at her.

"God made man and woman in His own image. We have a brain to think and choose what we want to do. If we choose God, then we'll want to be like Jesus. He came to show us how to live and love, and be kind to people, to be understanding. He even gave up His own life in place of ours; to die on a cruel, wicked cross. It's hard to imagine the excruciating pain He must have suffered as those huge nails were pounded deep into His hands and feet as He hung there; the weight of His body pulling with tortuous pain. He knew all He would have to say is, 'Father, please rescue me from this humiliation and suffering. I just can't take the terrible pain.' Instead, His love kept Him there. He cried out some of the most precious words, "Father forgive them for they do not know what they do." (Luke 23:34) Powerful words coming from our Savior."

"That's just a fairy tale; a bunch of nonsense," he scoffed. "I don't want to hear anymore of that crap."

"I'm sorry you feel that way. Jesus died for you, just as much as He died for me." Dawnelle's words were sincere. She started to say more, but he pushed her.

"Go on. Get out of here. I don't want anymore of that preaching stuff. You're just blabbering," he turned and pushed her out the door He had quickly opened.

Dawnelle didn't take time to say more. She ran down the hall to the stairs and quickly found her room, unlocked the door and grabbed the special cross lying on the counter. She touched up her disheveled hair, then promptly headed for the theater to find her family.

"Hey, where have you been? I was getting ready to come looking for you," Lance smiled. Then he noticed her stricken face. "Are you all right? You look a little shaken. Did something happen?"

She smiled and gave him a big hug. "I'll tell you later. I'm all right now that I'm with you, and all my family."

The songfest went according as scheduled. The group was at its best. Everyone knew this was the last night for the concert and gave them all the applause they could muster. It was very meaningful to Dawnelle, after what had happened to her. She felt very fortunate, since it could have been much worse. God is truly in control of every situation, especially when you put your trust in Him.

At the close of the concert, before they sang their usual closing hymn, Dawnelle asked to say a few words. She said, "I'd like to share one of my very favorite verses in the Bible, John 3:16 and I'd like to add the 17th verse that is very often left out, "For God so loved the world that He gave His only begotten Son, that whoever believes in Him should not perish but have everlasting life. For God did not send His Son into the world to condemn the world, but that the world through Him might be saved." Our God is a loving God. Have you ever wondered what it would be like to give up your own child? Many of us would give our own life rather than give up our child. That's how much God loves us. If you're not a Christian, please give some thought to what God did for you. He wants you in His Heaven, but you have to realize He can't accept sin in His world. So you need to give up those things that you know are not what God would have you do, and use the example that Jesus gave us; to Love one another as He has loved us. Our closing song tonight is 'For God So Loved the World.'"

They sang with sweetest harmony the words based on John 3:16 and asked the audience, who might know the hymn to join their voices with there's, as they sang it through once more. At the closing, Mr. C said a prayer. The audience was totally quiet, as he concluded the meaningful prayer with Amen and closed the service. Each one left the auditorium as if in awe, not wanting to speak, some with tears in their eyes.

Dawnelle couldn't help but look around to see if 'that man' was anywhere near. With a troubled heart, his presence wasn't seen. Still, she hoped he could have heard what she had shared. Maybe, just maybe, it might have penetrated his heart.

Backstage, she gathered her family together and expressed what had happened to her. They were all shocked, but thankful she was all right. Her parents and the young men lovingly reprimanded the girls for not telling them about the stalker earlier, and said they should have told them about their speculation about him.

Lance and Lyle insisted they would not leave their side for the rest of the trip.

The next morning, when everyone gathered to leave the ship, Dawnelle saw the man that brought such fear to her heart yesterday. He quickly rushed off the ship, looked back and saw Dawnelle. He raised his hands, with that familiar smirk on his face, threw something in the water close to shore. She glanced down and could see it was a Bible. Probably a Gideon Bible, she thought. It floated for a while with pages open, then slowly slipped out of sight.

Both girls looked at each other, shaking their heads. The man turned abruptly with a grin on his face. He didn't even look before he took a step backward. All of a sudden a shuttle bus pulled into the parking space as he stepped back, striking him. The man fell. There were screams of despair from the astonished crowd who saw what had happened. The bus driver heard the crowd yelling and motioning at the bus, and quickly hurried off the vehicle to check to see what he had hit. A security guard happened to be there. He checked the man, and shook his head at the bus driver, assuring him it was not his fault. They could hear people asking if he was dead. They could see the security guard nod his head and mouth his words, "Yes."

Tears came to Dawnelle's eyes. It was so sad when she saw him throw God's Word into the sea with no regret, only triumph showing on his face. Now...such a tragedy. Dawnelle realized that he didn't accept anything she had said to him.

Lance took her in his arms to comfort her.

CHAPTER SEVENTEEN

It was good to be home. Back to a life of love and comfort and familiarity. The cruise had been filled with adventure, embracing life in a different atmosphere with new things to do and see. But there's still something to be pleased with routine, and a loving, comfortable home.

Mr. C was back at the profession he enjoyed. Mrs. C took pleasure in being the caretaker of their lovely home and family. Cooking was her specialty. The girls loved and were proud of their positions at their father's business he had helped overcome some difficulties as a young man with lots of ideas, hopes, dreams.

Grant Collins didn't really start the cosmetic business. In fact, he had never thought he would be into cosmetics. The company was having a hard time…no real leadership…and was losing influence in the community. Grant Collins was an organizer and supervisor. He had a degree in business and was highly respected in the field of business, when asked to take on the position of CEO of the dying cosmetic company. It had taken several months of hard work and unfortunately some layoffs. But, soon, he was able to turn the company into a profitable business. He grew to love the challenge. Eventually, he bought the business.

The Taylor men were pleased to find their new business thriving under the care of Mrs. Arnold, the new secretary/ bookkeeper, and new mechanic, Joe Torrey. There were several appointments that needed to be checked out for scheduling on the list of sightseers desiring to capture the sights and sounds of the beautiful Pacific Northwest by helicopter.

There were several messages on the home answering machine, wanting the services of the popular quintet for upcoming dates, they would need to check out. The singing group enjoyed giving concerts, but didn't want to be too wrapped up in music as their main professions, although they found it exciting.

It wasn't until the end of the week when the six could get back together. Catching up on their job situations, while away, took priority time.

The Taylor twins had been invited for dinner on Friday evening.

"It seems like a month since we've seen you guys," Dawnelle greeted them at the door with a demure grin on her lovely face. The men appeared so good-looking, as they stood waiting patiently at the door. They were wearing slacks and sport shirts, always so neat and sharp looking, Dawnelle thought.

"Come in, come in!" Rochelle hurried to the door to greet them, when she heard their voices, pulling Lyle in. He grabbed her and gave her a warm kiss.

Lance smiled at Dawnelle, then took her in his arms. "I've missed you," was his greeting.

"Are the guys here?" Mrs. C's voice was heard coming from the kitchen. "Dinner will be ready in just a few minutes."

Mr. C made his way down the stairs, reaching out for the younger men's hands to greet them. "How are things going in the helicopter business? Did you find everything going well?"

"Yes, Sir," Lance spoke. "Our new employees did an excellent job of handling the business while we were gone. We have several trips lined up for the month."

"It looks like we have several singing engagements on the agenda also. We're going to need to check our schedules and see how to work them in our busy lives," Mrs. C said.

"I'm sure, with winter soon to be here, our sight seeing tours will slack off soon. We'll need to reach out and use the helicopters for other things," Lyle declared.

"We've been thinking about checking with the fire departments and see what we can do about using the helicopters and our abilities as search and rescue workers," Lance spoke up.

"There's probably a need for that type of work, I'm sure," Mr C encouraged. "The economy isn't the greatest right now. Still, it would be wise to talk to the City Council about using your skills for search and rescue in conjunction with the fire departments. I know some of the people on the council personally. I could see if we could set up an appointment with the council to consider this endeavor."

To see these two fine men desiring to expand their business was encouraging to Mr. C. If his daughters were as interested in possibly spending their lives with them, which appeared to him they were, he wanted to see them prosper and make a secure profession; one with which they could support a family.

The evening meal was delicious as usual. Everyone felt at ease to discuss the opportunities of their singing group, jobs, and responsibilities. Rochelle was catching up on some of the tasks at work that hadn't been done while she was away. Dawnelle was helping out one of her co-workers perfecting a fragrance for a new perfume. Mrs. C had been catching up on all the laundry from their trip, as well as spiffing up the house with autumn colors. After a while the parents started off to the television room to watch a favorite program, while the girls insisted on cleaning up the kitchen.

Both young men asked Mr. C if they could speak to him for a minute, to which the older gentleman readily agreed. Lyle wanted to join them.

Soon the two sets of twins were sharing and teasing each other. Lance gently captured Dawnelle's hands and raised them to his lips, took her aside, and spoke softly. "I have something for you in my pocket." He took out a small velvet box and handed it to her.

She looked up into his dreamy eyes, while accepting the gift. Quickly she opened it. Inside was a beautiful diamond ring surrounded with tiny emeralds. "Oh, it's exquisite." Her eyes were as large as a rose in bud beginning to spring open to full bloom.

Lance smiled, then said, "Dawnelle, I've been wanting to ask you for a long time. Will you marry me? I love you with all of my being. I want you to be my wife and mother of my children."

Tears began streaming down her cheeks. She looked at him with all the love flowing through her entire soul. "Oh, Lance. You're everything I could ever hope for in a husband; you're handsome; fun to be with; thoughtful and kind. I've loved you for a long time. Yes. Oh, yes, I would be honored to be your wife, and mother of our children."

Lance took her in his arms and said, "You've made me the happiest man alive, my beautiful darling."

"Hey! What's going on here?" A big grin appeared on Lyle's face.

"Dawnelle has just agreed to be my wife," Lance smiled at his brother.

Rochelle squealed, "I'm so happy for you two." The girls grabbed and hugged each other.

"Well, we might as well make it a double wedding," Lyle grinned at Rochelle.

"You want to marry me?" Rochelle looked at him, grinning.

"Of course, don't you want to marry me?" Lyle had a questioning expression on his face.

"You'll have to get down on your knee and propose, if you want me." Rochelle's face tried to appear stern.

"She's already being the boss," Lyle gave the impression of rejection.

"Well!" Rochelle waited with arms on her hips.

Finally, Lyle pulled her over to a comfortable chair, directed her to sit down. Then he got down on one knee, took her hands into his, and with a serious smile on his face, looked up into her dark brown eyes, waited a minute, then spoke, "Rochelle, I love you, and want you to marry me. Will you be my bride forever and always?"

"Forever and always I will be your bride. I have loved you ever since I saw your handsome face after leaving the hospital in Arizona, after you risked your life for me. Yes, yes, yes. I do want to marry you, my love."

Then Lyle took out a small velvet gift box from his pocket. He handed it to Rochelle, whose hands were trembling.

"It's similar to Dawnelle's, only it has sapphires surrounding the diamond. Please, put it on my finger," which he did.

"We've got to tell our wonderful news to Mama and Daddy," the girls both spoke at once. They ran to their folks, who were sitting in their reclining chairs absorbed in a favorite program.

"We're going to be married!" Both young women spoke the news at the same time.

"Well, it's about time," the mother smiled. Her eyes were all lit up, even though tears were streaming down her cheeks. "I thought I might never get to be a grandmother," She grinned.

The guys had followed their sweethearts to the TV room. The parents hugged all four of them, showing them how pleased they were with the announcement.

"I'm sure you haven't had time to set a date. With the holidays coming up soon, you'll have to decide if you want a Christmas wedding, or wait a while," Mrs. C's mind was already thinking ahead.

"Oooo, a Christmas wedding would be so beautiful, if you think it's not too soon to make all the plans," Dawnelle's expressive thoughts came out.

"We could do it if you want to, but there is a lot to do; sending out invitations, finding the right wedding dresses, or having them made. I'm sure you'll want to have a church wedding," Mrs. C looked up at her girls with a questioning look.

"Oh, yes." They both replied.

"I've always dreamed of a church wedding," Rochelle became dreamy eyed.

"Me too!" exclaimed Dawnelle in agreement.

"Tomorrow's another day. We'll start planning tomorrow," the mother said.

The three men all agreed, as Dad headed up the stairs toward bed. The Taylor men took the girls hands and aimed for the door. They didn't get far before the two couples embraced with obvious love in their eyes for each other.

CHAPTER EIGHTEEN

"Oh, my. So much to do and decisions to make: a date for the wedding; invitations to send out; finding our wedding dresses; where we will live." Dawnelle was standing in the kitchen talking to her mother and sister.

"Where we will live?" Rochelle looked stunned. "I always thought it would be fun to have my own home. Now, we have to decide where we will live. That's scary!"

Dawnelle looked at her sister, then her mother. "I hadn't thought about that. We wouldn't be living here with Dad and Mom, or each other. That is a little frightening. Makes me feel a little lonesome."

"Come on, girls. I know how you feel. I probably thought the same thing, when your father and I got married. You girls have two fine men to make a home with. It will be exciting. Some day you'll have children and will need a baby sitter, and I'll be available for you as much as possible. Well, I'm sure most of the time," the mother grinned. "Maybe you could find homes close by us, or close to the guys jobs. We'll still be able to get together on week-ends and holidays," she encouraged her daughters. Yet, in the back of her mind, she knew it would be lonely for her and her husband, once the girls moved to their own homes.

"There's some important decisions to be made. Whew!" Rochelle groaned. "We have a concert on Saturday. Let's get the guys together Saturday morning and discuss these things and the songs we would like to sing for our next concert."

"Good idea. The date of the wedding should be first, then we can really start organizing all the other things." Dawnelle agreed. "We'll need to get addresses for the invitations. We haven't met the guys brother or sister yet. We better get their addresses from the guys, and their other relatives addresses, as well as our own relatives.

Both future husbands came to the Collin's home early Saturday morning. They finalized their songs to sing for the concert, then discussed the wedding date. Since Christmas was on Monday this year, they decided to plan the wedding for the Friday evening following Christmas day; praying all their relatives would be able to make that date. The brothers were agreeable to contacting their brother and sister, and getting addresses for their other relatives to send the invitations. Some of their relatives lived in Arizona, as well as other parts of the United States. They talked about living in an apartment, if they couldn't find homes they liked. Now things were getting exciting. Finding an apartment shouldn't be too difficult.

Mother C called the church to check the date they had selected for the wedding. The date they had chosen was available, making them relieved and extremely happy.

Now, their dresses.

"Let's have them made," Rochelle suggested.

"Would you mind if I made them," Mother C spoke, with twinkles in her eyes.

138

"Could you? I know you have made many dresses for us through the years. But a wedding dress? That would be extremely difficult, wouldn't it?" Dawnelle smiled at her mother.

After a short pause, she smiled and said, "I would love to make them, if you don't choose a design too difficult."

"Oh, mother. Having you make our wedding dresses would be fabulous. Are you sure you would have the time?" Rochelle asked.

"We will help in any way we can." Dawnelle assured her.

The three women all hugged in agreement.

The guys elected to find a realtor to help them locate their ideal homes. Mr. C knew a good friend in the real estate business. He called her to set up an appointment with his prospective son-in-laws. At the same time, the women decided to go shopping for a dress pattern; then hopefully find the special material needed to sew the dresses.

They found a perfect dress pattern for their wedding. Each dress could be made a little different, yet very special. Dawnelle liked more lace then Rochelle. Rochelle wanted short sleeves, and Dawnelle wanted elbow length sleeves. Each dress would be just enough different to make them individual. Mother C assured them, with tears in her eyes, they would be beautiful. After some thought and discussion, a soft, white satin material was agreed upon, along with embroidered flowers of lace swatches to sew on wherever they desired. She wanted them to be dresses each girl would love.

Next on the agenda, after leaving the boutique, was to order the wedding invitations from the local printing company. Again, time was spent making decisions. The woman who waited on them assured the invitations would be ready in a couple weeks, or less. Believe it or not, the three women finally agreed on a lovely design. So far, two of their plans were falling in place. Soon they all returned home to get ready for the concert that evening. The next few days began a very hectic schedule. The women managed to work, model for their mother who had gotten started on her sewing project, address invitations, and still find time to practice for the next up-coming concert date two weeks away. All the work and planning had invigorated Mrs. C. She was the happiest her husband and children had seen her in years.

One evening Lance and Lyle took time after work to look over some property the real estate agent had found not far from where their helicopter business was presently located. It was a beautiful plot of land, twenty acres, with a river running near by, as well as a view of the King of the Cascade Mountain Range...Mt. Rainier, surrounded by much shorter peaks all stretching up to the heavens.

They made plans to view the property the following week-end with all the Collins' family.

When the men and women viewed the property, they were all thrilled. The men hadn't told the girls there was a house already on the property. It was a huge older home, but appeared to have been lovingly cared for. The building had many large windows overlooking the fabulous view of Mt. Rainier. They were thrilled with the lazy creek flowing near by. The house had a huge wrap around porch that covered three sides of the building. As one would walk in the front door, a generous sized room with a fireplace, made from white stones, filled the left side of the interior. The floor was native slate. As one would walk down the hallway of hardwood flooring, they discovered a small bathroom with an enclosed commode and sink and cupboard. A little farther down the hall they found a large bedroom with a large walk-in closet, and off to the right a nice sized bathroom with double sinks and lots of cupboards. To the right of the entrance into the house was a another large room with hardwood flooring, and to the back of it was a large modern kitchen with tile flooring and energy saving appliances. The refrigerator was huge, and two ovens took up nearly one wall. There was a pleasant sized eating space adjoining the kitchen. A nice sized laundry room was situated next to the kitchen area.

Four bedrooms, which would be adequate for queen sized beds, were found upstairs. They were pleased to find two large bathrooms separating the two bedrooms on both sides of the hallway with doors at each end to lock or share. At the end of the hallway was a fifth bedroom, fit for a king sized bed, running the entire width of the upstairs. A walk-in closet and a large bathroom adjoined the large room.

The yard was well landscaped with several fruit trees close by. Mother C noticed a nice sized garden with some raspberry bushes and strawberry plants overgrown with weeds. There were even some wild blackberries growing along a fence.

The brothers shared their ideas as to what they would like to do. What if they moved their helicopter business on to this land and construct a hanger with office space, and a pad for the helicopters? It would be situated at the back of the twenty acres. They would have to get permission from the city, county, state and federal authorities to build a launch pad for their helicopter business. All of this would, of course, take time, effort, and money. Their favorable perceptions felt it was perfect, if all the logistics fell into place. Would everyone be willing to take that chance?

The father reminding them it would take a lot of prayer and hard work, but there was no hesitation among the group to take that chance.

"Now, here's the biggest decision," Lance looked at each girl, "would you two ladies mind sharing the house together for a while after our wedding, until we could build the new houses you help us design? With the money we would be saving, if we rented two apartments, we could use making any needed repairs on this, umm, long established house, and buy the needed furniture for this charming house.

"Sure!" Both girl exclaimed, smiling at each other.

"It would be worth living together as newly weds," Rochelle grinned, shaking her head, yes.

The reply brought out sparkles of pleasure in the brother's eyes, as they winked at each other and grinned.

"This house reminds me of Aunt Nell and Uncle Myron's house, only much, much bigger," Rochelle exclaimed. "We used to spend a lot of our summers playing with all their animals: the milk cow and baby calves; the fifteen or more kittens they always seem to have; picking yummy peaches off the trees, and other fruit."

"Sometimes Aunt Nell would ask us to help her with a new project she wanted to create. I remember helping build a cement block wall on the hillside, and planting flowers she had grown from her greenhouse. I believe the old house is still there in Tacoma, even though she's been in Heaven for many years. She taught us so many things. What a sense of humor she had, always laughing at her own jokes. I've really missed her," Dawnelle thought out loud.

Aunt Nell was sister to their mother's grandmother. She never had children of her own, but loved the twins and enjoyed having them stay with her, especially after Uncle Myron died. She was so tiny, only weighing eighty-five pounds when she died...ten years following the death of her dear husband.

"You know what would be fun?" Rochelle shared. "We could make the house into a Bed and Breakfast."

"Yeh. We could turn it into a Victorian style. I've always loved antique furniture. Maybe we could find, and restore old furniture. We could go to garage sales around town, and auctions. I remember going to auctions with Aunt Nell and Uncle Myron. They were always finding such neat things." Dawnelle was dreaming, aloud.

"This sounds almost too good to be true," Rochelle excitedly spoke her thoughts.

"With God's help, we'll make it come true," Lance shared. He had such a believing heart and mind, Dawnelle thought to herself.

"God will always be our guide," Lyle agreed.

"You are two fine men. I'm proud to be your father-in-law…" Mr C said, adding, " to be," with a grin.

"Tomorrow we'll talk with Mrs. Huntley, our real estate agent and friend. She said she would correspond with an attorney she often worked with, to check into the possibilities of the helicopter business being accepted here." Lance informed them.

"We'll keep all these thoughts in our prayers. The Lord willing, He'll work things out for the good." Mr. C said. "In fact, let's say a prayer right now for God's leadership in this endeavor."

They all grabbed hands and bowed their heads, while Mr. C voiced a prayer for their coming undertakings. He was always such a praying man.

CHAPTER NINETEEN

The following week-end, the Taylor twins gave Mrs. Huntley a down payment on the property. Things looked encouraging about moving the helicopter business to the new property. The lay of the land was far enough from other homes, and yet close enough to be accessible to the public. The road was well paved and wide enough for local traffic. Also, it wasn't very far from where they had been renting their space for the current business they already were operating. The men were keeping busy in the business of transporting sightseers many places throughout the Pacific Northwest, as well as hauling some cargo for businesses near their work.

The girls wedding dresses were coming along beautifully. Mrs. C really enjoyed being the seamstress for the girls; always had. The wedding dresses were a bigger challenge than what she had expected them to be. Yet, she would never let her daughters know that. She wanted her girls to know she was putting her heart into every stitch, because they were sewed with love.

One evening, while the Collins' family was relaxing by the

fireplace in the living room, Dawnelle decided to share the thoughts she and her sister had been contemplating. She was a little reluctant, but needed to know how their parents would accept what they had been discussing.

"Daddy, would you feel bad if Rochelle and I decided to quit our jobs at the cosmetic company?" She paused to look at their Dad, then Mom.

The parents looked at each other, but didn't say a word.

"We have been so busy planning the wedding, wanting to find time to browse the antique shops for furniture, or go to auctions, and practice for concerts. It would be easier if we had more time to do all the things we need to do," Rochelle wanted to share her thoughts and support her sister.

Their Dad, looking over at his wife, finally spoke. He had a solemn look on his face. "You girls are very dear to us. Please know, we want what ever is best for you. If quitting your employment with the company would relieve some of the stress you girls are feeling, of course you should do so. You both have been an added bonus to the company, I must add, but we will find someone to fill your positions, even if it will be tough," he released a grin. "The company will survive. You are so special, each one of you, to us and to the company."

Both girls embraced their parents with big hugs.

"We are so excited about our wedding and turning the house into a Victorian style Bed and Breakfast," Rochelle spoke.

"Mama, you're going to have to teach us some cooking instructions before we open up our new business. We'll have to specialize on gourmet breakfast recipes." Dawnelle said.

"You know what we should do? We'll need to convince the men to take us to different places for our honeymoons, and stay in Bed and Breakfasts to help give us ideas on specializing on this kind of business," Rochelle proposed.

"Good idea," the mother agreed.

"Hmm, I would like to go to Hawaii on our honeymoon," Dawnelle projected a dreamy look about her.

Rochelle then shared her thoughts, "I'm going to see if Lyle will take me to New York and see Niagra Falls."

"Ohh, that's awesome, too. If we stayed in Bed and Breakfasts, that would give us ideas from different parts of the country," was Dawnelle's thoughts. Then she said, "We'll give the company two week's notice tomorrow, if that's okay, Daddy?" She looked at her father with a sad, but questioning ambience.

Dad asked, with a long face, "Have you girls thought about taking a leave of absence, or do you want this to be a resignation? Whatever my lovely daughters' desire is what I want," the father assured them.

They both decided it was best to resign.

The two weeks went by fast. Dawnelle's good friend and co-worker, Terryli, the one who would replace Dawnelle in the cosmetic business, felt they had found the right ingredients for the new fragrance they had been working on. It was a musky smell with an exotic pleasure.

Terryli had become engaged to her boyfriend over the week-end, and was bubbling over with joy. The two had been dating for ages. She thought her boyfriend would never propose. Now, she couldn't quit smiling. So, they both decided each one would try the new perfume on their fiances' that evening to see what kind of reaction they would have.

Lance, teasingly, kept sniffing Dawnelle's neck for the special smell all evening. When he was asked if he liked the fragrance, he would look at her and plug his nose. She just lightly swatted him on his back side.

Rochelle was training one of the girls she had made good

friends with in the office to take over her position. Lynda was the trainee, thrilled to be taking on a more enjoyable task, since she had been the "gopher" for the department. She felt the new job would give her a more prestigious position in the company and was thrilled with the advancement.

Both twins' emotions were a bit torn to be leaving the cosmetic plant. It was something they had wanted to do all their growing up years...being a part of their father's business. Still, a new light was flickering. An exciting challenge lay before them. Being married to the sweetest, kindest, thoughtful, extraordinary men in the world could only be fantastic. And...having a new business of their own, looked to show a potential.

"Oh, oh!" Dawnelle shook her head, really speaking to herself. Mama had always warned them not to put people upon a pedestal. Mom said it wasn't fair to the person, or to yourself. People are just human and make mistakes. We need to be aware of that, and allow them, well, one or two mistakes anyway. She smiled to herself. Still, she couldn't imagine Lance would ever make a mistake, or do anything erroneous.

Lance and Lyle didn't show up for their concert practice on Saturday, as they usually did. The girls finally decided their fellows must have gotten too busy and didn't think to call their mother to let her know they wouldn't be able to come. She had fixed one of her special dinners just for them, everything they liked: barbeque ribs, baked potatoes, corn on the cob, etc., and a peach cobbler for dessert.

Rochelle tried calling them, both at their apartment and business. No answer. They knew Mrs. Arnold, their office manager, wouldn't be there in the office on a Saturday. Still, they hoped maybe at least one of the guys would answer their call.

Well, their next concert wasn't until the following Saturday evening, but still, Dawnelle was a little "put out" with them for not at least calling to let them know they weren't coming.

The phone was ringing off the hook the next day, when Mrs. C hurried into the kitchen to respond to the persistent ringing of the phone after church on Sunday.

It was Lyle. "Sorry, Mrs. C for not calling yesterday. Unfortunately, we were in an accident. Lance is still in the hospital. Well, we both are for now. Lance has dislocated his shoulder, and has a sprained ankle. He should be able to leave for home this afternoon. The doctor wanted to keep us both overnight last night for observation, because of possible head injuries. We both had been knocked out, even though we were wearing seat belts and helmets, when the helicopter hit the ground. We had been unconscious for a couple hours before the Park Rangers found us. Please let the girls know we'll be all right. I don't know what condition the helicopter is in right now."

"I am so sorry, Lyle. We'll come and get you as soon as you both can be released," Mrs. C's voice was filled with concern. "Where are you?"

"We're in the Wenatchee hospital," he answered.

"Oh, so far? Please say you'll come and stay with us until you feel better." Mother C said.

"Are you sure you don't mind?" He sounded relieved.

"Of course we don't mind. We want you," she assured him.

"What's wrong, Mom?" Both girls spoke at once, as they gathered around their mother. They had overheard the one sided conversation and were anxious to find out what had happened,

Mrs. C told Lyle good-bye, and stressed to him again to call just as soon as they could leave. She gave him their cell phone number. Then she repeated to the family what Lyle had conveyed to her.

"Oh, Mama, let's go to the hospital now," Rochelle quickly said. "I know it will take time to drive over the Cascades, but we must see them. Tears were running down both girls faces.

All four of the Collins' family grabbed their coats and purses, then headed out immediately for the hospital in Wenatchee. It was several hours before they located the hospital. Mr. C immediately went to the Admissions Office, to see if he could check the young men out of the hospital. In spite of the accident, there were smiles on their handsome, yet bruised faces, when they spotted the Collins' women walking through the door of their room. Both men were sitting in wheelchairs waiting for them. Neither one were in the usual good form they were used to seeing. The two couples gave each other loving kisses, Mom, too. When Dad got there, he carefully gave them a long hug with their release papers in his hand. Two nurses were following right behind Mr. C with wheel chairs, ready to wheel them to the Collins' SUV.

"Mom, Dad, it's getting so late. Why don't we find a Bed and Breakfast tonight? Maybe we can get some ideas for our own Bed and Breakfast," Dawnelle proposed.

"If the patients feel well enough," the mother looked back at the two young men. They both had droopy eyes. "Looks like they need to get some more rest. Okay with you Grant?"

"Sure. I'll call in early in the morning to let my secretary know I won't be in for work tomorrow."

"Let's go to Leavenworth. That's my favorite little Bavarian town," Rochelle suggested.

On the way to Leavenworth, the young men relayed what

had happened to them. There was a problem with the helicopter they were flying. When they realized they were losing power and found the fuel gauge showing empty, they started lowering the chopper to land. Lance called the FAA control tower in Seattle to give them their location, and that they were having problems. All of a sudden the chopper just plopped down. It had landed so hard they both knocked their heads on something, causing them to lose consciousness, even though they were in seat belts and wearing helmets. The next thing they knew, two Forest Rangers had found them and were pulling them out of the chopper, ready to take them aboard a waiting ambulance to the nearby hospital on Saturday evening.

During their stay in the hospital, a couple inspectors from the FAA located the helicopter and did a thorough inspection. They wrote their input on what was wrong, but waited for the company mechanic's report before finalizing their part of the official examination.

Joe Torrey, their lead mechanic, had been contacted by Lyle early Sunday morning to get to their chopper. He had instructions from the FAA in Seattle of where to find the helicopter. Joe arrived at the scene later on Sunday afternoon. He knew he needed to find the trouble quickly. His findings were reported to the FAA in Seattle, which was the fuel line's connection had come loose, causing the chopper to run out of fuel. Joe apologized over and over again to his two employers, because he blamed himself for not finding the loose connection before they flew the vehicle. All knew and agreed with the FAA, a loose fuel line was the problem. It couldn't have been loose when they took off. Somehow it became loose in flight.

The brothers had both been on board, because it took both of them to unload the supplies they had flown to a Ranger Station on the east side of the Cascades. It was a heavy load. They had left early Saturday morning. They felt they would have enough time to distribute the supplies, which they did, and still make it to the Collins' home for dinner that night. Unfortunately, they were both knocked unconscious, because of the hard landing, and were transported to the hospital instead.

Thankfully, the helicopter received only a few dents and scratches. Joe repaired the fuel line, and he would be able to fly the chopper back to Seattle. However, not until the following week, if FAA approved of the evaluations and repair job. Which they did.

Leavenworth was not far from Wenatchee. It was well lit up with lovely lights throughout the small town, as if welcoming them to the quaint city situated in the Cascade mountains. A light snow had fallen during the evening. Mr. C stopped at a gas station for fuel. While there he asked if the employee knew of a Bed and Breakfast in town. It just so happened his aunt and uncle owned and operated one not far off the main street, therefore he was able to give them directions. It was a lovely, older home with a big sign saying, "Welcomen Inn," with Bed & Breakfast under the sign, and a Vacancy sign under it.

Being Sunday night, many of the visitors in town had left for their own homes in other cities, and their jobs tomorrow. But there were still many tourists buzzing in and out from one tempting gift shop to another, excited to find one last gift from "the old world." A large number of buildings had scenes of mountains, forests, and rivers painted on the fronts of their buildings. Colorful baskets of flowers hung from their eaves. The style of the buildings reminded the guests of Switzerland, or at least what people often thought Switzerland must look like from pictures they had seen. Not far from the B & B was a river flowing swiftly close by.

Before settling in to their rooms, everyone decided they'd

better eat something. It had been a long day and getting late. After checking with their host, they walked the short distance to town where they found the exquisite restaurant he had recommended, and were seated at a lovely table next to a cozy stone fireplace. The menu was of select German food. Everyone enjoyed the scrumptious food. A woman dressed in a colorful Swiss outfit strolled by, singing some old songs, sharing her yodeling talent, while they took pleasure in their delightful meal.

After awhile, Mrs. C noticed the men were exhausted, so they all agreed to head back to the B & B. After finding their bedrooms upstairs in the lovely home, the men were ready to enjoy the comfort of the antique style beds with soft feather pillows and pillow top mattresses. Each set of twins shared a room, with a double bed for the girls, twin beds for the guys. They would need to share a bathroom at the end of the hallway, however. The parents claimed the master bedroom with their own bathroom.

Mr. C smiled and said how nice to have the quiet and peace of the mountains with the river to sing them to sleep. Everyone was tired. Well, except for the girls. They just had to spend a few minutes browsing the gift shops, if they were still open. Maybe they could find something for their new house. Mom C had to agree, and went along. It didn't take but a few minutes for the three women to walk towards town. Soon after they left, it didn't take but a few minutes for the three men to climb in their own beds for a much needed rest.

After quickly peaking into some of the shops, the girls found a House of Clocks. It was there they debated over an ornately crafted, grandfather clock. Unfortunately, it was too big to transport in the car. If they really desired to purchase the clock, the owner of the shop said he could ship it the next week to their home. That cinched the sale. Mother C said she would buy it as a wedding gift for the Taylor families new home/business. The girls were thrilled and couldn't wait to tell their guys, who they found sound asleep when they peaked into their bedroom. The girls were good, though. They waited until the following morning after breakfast to share the news of the exquisite gift their mother had purchased for them.

Breakfast! What a delight! Everyone was starved, just looking at the food. Warm applesauce muffins, fruit juices, as well as scrambled eggs and Canadian bacon, and plenty of hot coffee and hot chocolate were sitting on the large table, when everyone arrived from their upstairs bedrooms. What a treat! The aroma was tantalizing in itself. Their hosts were smiling and very accommodating.

"We'll surely have to remember this when we have our own Bed and Breakfast," Rochelle exclaimed, full of enthusiasm.

The trip home was very pleasant. The Taylor twins were feeling much better after the restful nights sleep. Moving around without too many aches and pains was much appreciated. Teasing one another was back, and presented an enjoyable and amusing time for their travel home to the other side of the Cascades.

CHAPTER TWENTY

Thanksgiving Holiday is drawing near. There were so many things to be thankful for. Closing on the house and buying property for the new business for the Bed and Breakfast has been approved. The final legal papers have been signed for permission to start building the hanger for the helicopter, landing pad and offices for the Taylor's helicopter business. Ever since the guys had put the down payment on the property, the girls have been spending their money they had earned from employment at their father's business, buying furniture for the B & B.

The guys decided to move in to their new house as soon as possible. Their present abode, the apartment, had been furnished. Finding the right furniture for the new home was a necessity now. Of course the girls have been searching all the antique shops, and dragging their men to auctions as time allowed. Quite a bit of furniture has already been acquired. Once moved, the guys felt they could spend the evening hours and week-ends building the hanger, chopper pad, shop, and office.

It would give the girls more time to complete some of the restoring work on the furniture they had purchased. Several pieces the girls have refurbished with an excellent restoring finish product that was recommended by the antique shops.

The gift Mom had purchased in Leavenworth, the huge, expensive grandfather clock was the first piece of furniture to arrive at the new home. A special place in the living room area across from the white stone fireplace was agreed on. As the refurbished furniture was finished each piece was placed in their new home in just the perfect spot as well.

Besides the grandfather clock, the girls found an 1880's piece of furniture, a "fainting sofa" of red velvet and oak wood, perfect for the living room. A small oak table with a marble top, all set for a chess game or checkers, and two small matching oak chairs were set at one of the large windows in the living room overlooking a view of the small stream flowing by. A beautiful sawn oak, round table with four chairs was seated in the breakfast nook off the kitchen at the back of the house. A pleasing view overlooking the small orchard of fruit trees could be enjoyed while eating.

An ornately carved China buffet was selected for the large dining area. It had several drawers for silverware. There were two large cupboards with shelves for napkins and table cloths with ornately carved doors. Attached to each side of the buffet were sentimental shelves enclosed in glass for special knick-knacks. There was a glassed in area on the top with several shelves for dishware. Beautiful dishes had been found in the attic of their parents home, which they had recovered from the estates of their grandmother and Aunt Nell when they had died. The dishes looked beautiful in the huge buffet, which fit in the large dining room perfectly. Now they needed to search for a large table that would seat ten people to accommodate the expected clientele, as well as compliment the newly purchased buffet. They would still have room for two smaller tables in the room, if they needed more seating space.

Since the guys were moving in, it was decided one couple would claim the master bedroom upstairs, the other couple would claim the bedroom downstairs; with the flip of a coin the decision was made. They decided each couple would decorate their own bedroom. Each agreed everything in the house must be of a Victorian or early American style. The guys really didn't care, but tried not to show it. What was chosen and where it was placed, with their help of course, was left up to the girls. Whatever furniture and arrangements they chose, just needed to be comfortable, was the men's desire.

Furniture for six bedrooms, plus a sofa and some chairs for the living room were needed. The two large bedrooms would be the bedrooms for the two couples after they married. Since the guys wanted to move in right away, this would take top priority. The pursuit was in full swing as they were adding to the adventure of furnishing their B & B. So far, all of their recently chosen furniture had been ornately carved from a turn of the century American oak design, making them full of enthusiasm.

One day both girls were mesmerized when they walked into an antique shop. Right over the counter at the entrance of the store hung the most fantastic chandelier they had ever seen. It was very large. Four tiers of gold and crystal with many shining lights were sparkling up the entrance to the store.

"Isn't it the most elegant antique we could ever find?" Dawnelle exclaimed.

"Oh, yes, it would be perfect in the dining room," Rochelle quickly agreed.

A line of customers graced the counter with their purchases in hand, so the girls stood in line several minutes before they could get information about the chandelier. They were so excited, it was hard to wait, but their time finally came. Two ladies were at the counter to help them with big grins on their faces. They could tell the twins were bubbling over with excitement as they kept exclaiming and pointing to the lamp over their heads.

Dawnelle finally asked if the light fixture was for sale, since there was no price tag hanging from the lamp. Both ladies said they didn't know, but with a grin, said for the right price, they looked at each other and agreed, it probably could be purchased. One of the ladies said the owner of the store had recently acquired the lovely fixture from an old hotel that was being torn down for a parking garage.

"Is the owner of the shop here?" Rochelle asked.

"I'm sorry. He's away for a few days, but we can take your information and have him contact you, if you're really interested," the sales clerk suggested.

"Oh, we're interested," both girls quickly spoke.

At once, Rochelle found a tablet in her purse and wrote down their names, address and phone number. Both girls thanked the clerks for their help, and walked out the entrance of the store entranced, as they glanced back at the beautiful piece of majesty hanging above the counter one more time.

It was a couple days before the phone call came through from the owner of the antique shop. He introduced himself as Charles Bennett. He was very friendly and thoughtful, as he spoke with the girls listening over the speaker phone. When they shared what they planned to do with such a large chandelier, he was quite interested. They told him about the Bed and Breakfast. He seemed very pleased, then shared the background of the lighting fixture. The hotel he had purchased it from was very old, and had not been in service for many years. When he learned the building was to be demolished, he immediately thought of the chandelier he had admired for so many years, and decided immediately to purchase it, although he, himself, didn't have a place to hang it. He felt sure someone would be pleased to buy it, so he had it cleaned and rewired for safety reasons, then hung it in his antique store just a few days ago. Many people had inquired about it, but felt it was too big for them to purchase, although they really admired the magnificent fixture.

"I'm very pleased you want it for your new venture," Mr. Bennett spoke with sincerity.

They agreed on a reasonable price. Then he said he would, himself, bring it to their house, and would even hang it, if that would meet their approval. His main career was as an electrician, but had retired from that profession. After obtaining so many antiques through the years, he decided to open his own antique store Mr. Bennett seemed very interested in viewing the house they were turning into a Bed and Breakfast. He even commented, if he heard of anyone who would like to enjoy th Bed and Breakfast, he would give them their location. "Did they have any business cards?" He asked.

Dawnelle had to tell him, no, but they would be sure they would send him some as soon as they had them designed. A new friend was made that day.

By the end of the week, the fabulous chandelier was hanging over the location where a dining room table would be placed. Mr. Bennett was very pleased with the obvious work of love the two sets of twins had accomplished with the older home. He promised he would let them know of any other piece of antiques he may come across that they might like to add to their possessions.

Dad and Mom decided to give each of their daughters early

wedding gifts. The parents had purchased stock in the cosmetic company for the girls trust funds, and added to them, as the twins were growing up. Now it was time to sign the legal papers, to allow them to cash them in, or part of them, if they wanted to use the money to purchase furniture or any amenities for their new home. The two young couples couldn't thank the parents enough for such a thoughtful gift. How fortunate they felt to have such loving parents.

The Collins' decided it would be exciting for the Taylor twins' brother and sister and their families to stay in the house during the days before the wedding, even though they might not be completely finished. Also, one of their aunt and uncle's have expressed to the young men their desire to come to the wedding. The aunt was sister to their mother, who had died in the plane crash several years earlier. The nephews were so pleased they wanted to come to their wedding. Both sets of twins desired for them to stay in the big house, also.

That would mean they would need to furnish five empty bedrooms upstairs, as well as the one downstairs. So, the challenge was, by Christmas time, they wanted to have the furniture they needed in place to provide for their special guests until after the wedding.

"Oh, can't you just see our lovely new home all decorated for Christmas?" Rochelle exclaimed.

"It will be so much fun to decorate the house ourselves, inside and out. We could start our own traditions," Dawnelle had that dreamy look again. "I'm eager to meet Lance and Lyle's brother and sister and their families, as well as their Aunt Edith and Uncle Charlie. I sure hope all the family members will like each other."

Rochelle agreed, then proclaimed, "First things first, we must find the bedroom furniture."

"Someone at church mentioned to me last Sunday about a popular antique store in Sumner.

Why don't we drive there tomorrow and check it out." Mother C suggested.

Wednesday the three women found the huge warehouse and were thrilled with all the lovely antiques they discovered. They found two king sized bedroom outfits which had bed frames, a chest of drawers, and huge dressers with mirrors all ornately carved in American oak. Three smaller dressers and queen sized beds with matching dressers, were found, along with a twin bedroom outfit and a small dresser; these would complete the bedroom furniture for the six bedrooms in their lovely, older home. One of the outfits was painted a pale green with flowers and beautiful designs. They all agreed it was absolutely lovely for one of the guest rooms.

Mother C reminded them that they hadn't looked for living room furniture yet. Right away, Dawnelle spied an extraordinary sofa that would be just a perfect match for the "fainting chair" already purchased. It was of a thickly brocaded material in red, with three ornately curved backs and pleasingly soft seating. Two comfortable stuffed chairs of a light brown leather in an early American style were chosen for the completion of the living room furniture. The friendly sales clerk said the furniture could be delivered by the end of the week. The ladies were all thrilled with the purchases. Mom was equally as excited with their choices as her daughters were. While directing the car towards home, it was decided to pick up some burgers and fries for dinner. Rochelle called the Taylor twins by cell phone on the way home to invite them to share in the dinner, that way they could share their shopping experience.

Now, the desire is to open the Bed and Breakfast to the public as soon as possible, after celebrating Thanksgiving Day, a special concert for Christmas, Christmas Day, the wedding, honeymoon, and bringing in of the New Year.

Well, maybe by…February…..?

The week before Thanksgiving, the furniture had been delivered and set up in the bedrooms. New pillow top mattresses had been ordered for all the beds, but would be next Monday before they could be delivered. The sofa was a perfect match for their special lounging chair in the living room.

They found one of the families at church was wanting to part with an old antique table. It had been in their family for years. But it was just too big for the new house they had moved into recently. When the girls saw it, at first they were disappointed. It was oak, and it did have ten chairs that matched the table. However, everything was in rather bad shape. They didn't want to hurt the people's feelings. They looked at each other, covered their face with their hands and frowned as they looked away. But Lance looked it over carefully, and decided the table just needed some tender loving care and be lovingly restored to it's original condition. The chairs needed new cushions to replace the stained ones, otherwise the set was solid and very usable. Their decision was to buy the outfit. After the work of restoration during the rest of the week, the table and chairs fit in the dining room perfectly, and became a pleasing part of the dining room. As well, the chandelier could make anything look lovely; and it certainly did.

Thanksgiving Day was a day of rest. Well, more for the guys. The usual meal of turkey and dressing, sweet potatoes, mashed potatoes, a green bean casserole, Waldorf salad, croissants, homemade jams and jellies, pumpkin and pecan pies, hot apple cider was put together for the delicious meal by the three ladies. Dad expressed the family prayer, thanking God for all the blessings throughout the year. He asked each one to share one special blessing each had received this year. Each individual shared their special thoughts, then said it was hard to limit it to only one. God had truly been gracious to everyone. The ladies were happily pleased with all the gracious compliments from their men over the meal. They were glad when the leftovers were stored for snacks as needed. The good dishes were washed and put away for the next holiday. Of course the men were enjoying watching football games, that took most of their day, in between "having to" snack on all the scrumptious food the women had prepared.

The following Saturday was decoration day for both sets of twins. A special tree was found towards the back of their property. It was going to have to be cut down anyway, since it would be in the way of the helicopter pad. They had bought bags and bags of all kinds of Christmas decorations to decorate all through the house, and lighting for all around the outside of the wrap-around porch. Mom gave them some of the decorations the girls had made through the years to place on the large Christmas tree that had been set up in the living room.

Lyle mentioned that their family didn't take time to do much decorating. Their mother, a registered nurse, worked many of the holidays at the hospital. A lot of the time their father was flying across country getting passengers to their destinations for the holidays. Sometimes they just ate at a restaurant for their special dinner. So, this was all new to them; the decorating that is. But they seemed to enjoy helping their sweethearts with hanging the decorations. They teased and shared with each other, while singing along with Christmas carols played on the CD player. Garlands and red bows were hung along the stairway leading upstairs. The fireplace was decorated with silk poinsettias and greenery with four big red stockings hanging down from the mantel.

Dawnelle didn't notice that Lance had hung an angel ornament on her pony tail, until Lyle tried to hang a Mrs. Santa ornament on Rochelle's sweatshirt. Pretty soon they were chasing each other inside the house: upstairs, downstairs, outside, until they became so exhausted. Finally, they laughingly decided they had better stick to decorating the remainder of the tree. Soon, lights were hung out on the railing around the huge porch…with green garlands to add that special effect. A manger scene was placed, all lit up with lights on the front lawn, reminding visitors of the "Reason for the Season." Lance and Lyle even set up recorded music of Christmas carols to be heard, as people reached the front porch.

During the family conversations lately, it was mentioned, if anyone asked what kind of wedding gifts should their family and friends might want to buy for the newly-to-be wed couples, tell them towels and bedding. Yet, they could use most anything for their Bed and Breakfast.

Early in December the church gave the two sets of twins a wedding shower. Dawnelle commented, "I think nearly every member of the church was there." They received so many nice gifts, from bedding, to towels, appliances for the kitchen, intricate doilies made by some of the older ladies, some beautiful pictures for the walls, even one by Thomas Kincaid, lovely table cloths, just anything and everything they received could be used somewhere. The girls, and guys, were thrilled with all the very thoughtful and lovely gifts. They had fun finding just the right location to place each special item.

Another wedding shower was given by the girls from the Girl Scout troop the twins had been leaders for earlier in the year. In the fall, Dawnelle and Rochelle had felt they didn't have the time to carry on as leaders for the girls and give them the leadership they deserved. Although the girls were disappointed the twins had resigned their positions, they were still having fun and caring for the people in the nursing home, as well as learning new challenges to becoming fine young ladies. Serena's mother, Mary, had taken on the troop, and was doing an exceptional job with them. The girls had put together recipe booklets of their favorite foods for their presents to give to their two favorite couples. Each had helped make a large spice rack as a gift for their kitchen. It was beautifully painted and decorated with silly little pictures of fruits and vegetables, and filled with all kinds of spices. Mary said they had so much fun making their gifts. Each one was so precious to the twins. A special place was found in the kitchen for the spice rack. Their new home was really taking on a family atmosphere. Both girls exclaimed several times how exciting it will be when they could move in. Since the mattresses had been delivered, the guys had moved their personal stuff in and was living there in the their bedrooms…. "In their big house all alone," the guys would say to the girls, with pitiful eyes."

CHAPTER TWENTY-ONE

It's just a few days before the wedding. Everyone has been so busy. The Christmas concert at church was beautiful on Sunday. The quintette had been part of the program; singing a medley of Christmas songs. Excitement kept building even though nerves were crashing into one another.

Lamps and a coffee table and several small tables, have been purchased and placed by the sofa and chairs, adding to the comfort of the living room. Beds had all been made up for their guests. The gifts of doilies, and pictures have been hung and placed around in each room for that special inviting affect. Everything in the newly purchased house was as ready as it could be.

The girls had also helped their parents decorate their house for Christmas. Decorating had always been a fun time for the family, and the girls didn't want their parents to feel left out.

Lance and Lyle's relatives were arriving at Sea-Tac airport tomorrow. Their aunt and uncle, brother and sister and their families will be here. Their first guests for the new Bed and Breakfast will be family. How special!

Leslie Collins was in her glory. Her specialty was cooking. Since the guests would all be arriving by early evening the following day, she had convinced the Taylor twins to bring their guests to the Collins' home for the evening dinner. Give them time to freshen up and settle in at the Bed and Breakfast before they come, she stated. The refrigerator and freezer had been filled with easy to cook meals and condiments at the big house, but they wouldn't feel like cooking on traveling day. Eating out could get "old" after awhile, was her thoughts.

They were all feeling a little nostalgic. Mom caught herself feeling tears ready to fall at any minute. And yet, she was so pleased with her daughters' choice of young men to marry. She already felt like they were a part of the family. The "boys" she never could have.

The daughters helped Mom prepare the meal for their company: making pies, a large salad, peeling potatoes, and anything and everything they could do to help. All of their lives would be changing in just a short amount of time. The parents would be all alone once their only offsprings would be married. They wouldn't be far from each other, but it would be so different. Then, those tears silently began to fall.

A knock on the front door was heard from the kitchen, where the three women had been finishing the last minute preparations for dinner. The table had already been set with the fine china. Grant answered the door with a happy smile on his face. "Come in! Come in!" he motioned to the small crowd of visitors.

Uncle Charlie showed a huge grin on his face, as he escorted his lovely wife in the doorway, and introduced himself and his wife, Edith. Jack, the older brother, a reflection of the twins, grabbed his outstretched hand and entered next. He introduced himself and his wife, Lavena.

"Hi, I'm Margie, the twins' sister," the young woman said, while directing a squirming little boy to the door. "Our little guy's name is Lamar, he's five." Her husband, was carrying a very shy little girl in his arms right behind his wife. She was introduced as Katelynn. She's four years old. I'm, Tyler he told them.

Lance and Lyle came in last with big grins on their faces.

"These starving people couldn't wait to get here. We told them about Mrs. C's great cooking." Lyle proclaimed.

Mrs. C had arrived at the door by this time with a happy smile on her face.

Rochelle and Dawnelle appeared a little shy, but shown expressions of happiness on their faces. The Taylor twins didn't appear shy at all. They embraced their fiances' and kissed them right there, passionately, in front of everyone. Then both spoke at the same time, "Aren't they beautiful?" Then they introduced their lovely ladies to their family members.

"Dawnelle is the one who turns my darkness into light," said Lance, as he watched his special one turn as red as the poinsettias sitting in decorated pots on each side of the front door.

No more shyness was noticed the rest of the evening. Conversation was finding out about everyone: what they did, where they lived, how long could they stay, and so on. They were all a very lively bunch of dear people. Everyone soon felt very much at home and welcome. The Collins' were all thrilled to be enjoying each family member.

The dinner was the best.

Each of the couples wanted to go shopping for gifts. They

had decided to wait until they saw their twins new house to see what they might need.

Leslie told the women she would take them shopping the following morning. Edith, the young couples aunt, was very close to Leslie's own age. They had made friends right away, and found they liked many of the same things. She found Edith to be a real helper in the kitchen, and had offered to help with any of the preparations for the wedding as she could.

Rochelle suggested she could take Margie and Lavena shopping with Dawnelle, if they would like. They decided that would be a good idea, so they could get to know each other even better. "I'm sure the guys would be glad to take care of the children," Rochelle grinned at Lyle.

He grinned and accepted the suggestion.

In no time at all, it seemed, the company was heading for the front door for their nights' rest. It would still be a couple days before the wedding.

After breakfast the next morning, the families got together at the Collins' household. Katelynn and Lamar spied the tire swing in the backyard that Mr. C had hung up in one of the trees. He saw Katelynn was already trying to climb onto the tire. Mr. C walked outside to help her in the swing. Once in, she hung on for dear life, with a grin as big as a Cheshire cat. Uncle Charlie threw a ball to his nephew, Lamar, who was disappointed he didn't get to the swing first; soon the ball distracted his unhappy face. It wasn't long until they found the other toys the Collins had purchased for the kids to play with while they were here.

The Taylor twins and brother, Jack, and brother-in-law, Tyler, soon took over the babysitting chores.

The women headed out in two separate cars for their shopping spree. It wasn't long until the two older men found the coffee pot and grabbed their coats and a patio chair to watch the children, wishing they had as much energy as those little ones. The four younger men decided to go back inside the house to find a ball game on TV, since they had been relieved of their duties.

Edith asked Leslie if she thought the young couples would like some furniture for the front porch of their new business adventure. Leslie felt the furniture would be greatly appreciated. She knew just the perfect store to do their shopping. They found two comfortable looking antique rockers and a glider swing that would seat two that looked perfect for gifts. Edith didn't know which ones to purchase, so she decided to buy all three pieces.

"Oh, you don't have to buy all three," Leslie grinned.

"Those two boys have always been so special to us. If you think they will all like the furniture, that's what Charlie and I want to do," she smiled.

"Knowing both young couples, I'm sure they will be more than pleased," Leslie assured her.

The glider was in a big box and would have to be assembled. It slid into the back of the SUV, after the seats had been collapsed for room. The two rocking chairs barely fit in, but they made it.

"I guess that takes care of our shopping trip," both women laughed.

The four younger ladies were having fun with their shopping as well. Margie and Lavena found a couple lovely table cloths for the long table in the dining room that should fit perfectly. One was a white lace cloth, the other was of a delightful Christmas design. They both had already bought a gift before they had left home. But they couldn't resist buying the table cloths.

Of course the twins always find something to add to their

new home, whenever they go shopping. They were also having such fun showing their new relatives "to-be" some of the sights of Seattle. They finally said, let's go to the Space Needle for lunch. It's on us.

Lavena was a little apprehensive about the height, but she didn't want to spoil the fun for the rest of the group, so she didn't say anything. By the time they reached the top of the Space Needle, her complection was white as snow.

"Oh, Lavena, are you going to faint on us?" Dawnelle noticed Lavena's appearance right away, and grabbed her shoulders to hold her.

"I'm sorry. I should have told you I have a fear of heights." She was so embarrassed. "I didn't want to spoil your fun."

"We're so sorry," Rochelle smiled her loving smile. "We'll go right back down and find another place to eat for lunch."

There was another special restaurant the girls enjoyed, so they took their group there instead. Lavena's color was back to normal. They had a marvelous time sharing their thoughts and taking pleasure in one another's company.

The twins had written and asked if Katelynn could be their flower girl for the wedding, and Lamar their ring bearer. Margie was so pleased for them to want their children to be a part of the wedding, and assured them Tyler was pleased, too. They had decided Christmas colors would be perfect for their outfits, but decided to wait until they got to Seattle to buy the clothes. They wanted the girls to help her pick out the style and colors appropriate for the special occasion.

So, after several stores, Margie finally found a darling red dress for her daughter. It was full of ruffles and lace. Then she found the cutest navy blue outfit for her son, and a white shirt and a red bow tie to finish his outfit. The twins were thrilled with Margie's choice of clothes for the children. They went to a wedding shop to find a beautiful pillow to carry both wedding ring sets for the double wedding. A beautiful white basket was also found for their little flower girl.

They all agreed to stop and buy four large pizza's for the evening meal that night. Dawnelle assured them there was probably enough leftovers to finish up the rest of the meal. They all agreed.

The men were all surprised when the shoppers all walked into the front door of the Collins' home. They really expected to have to carry a lot more bundles of goodies in from the cars. 'Course Mrs. C said what she had in her car could wait to be unloaded until after dinner, since she knew the guys were probably starved, and they needed to unload the goods at the B & B.

No argument could be heard.

The pizzas were set on the table, as the ladies got out more food from the kitchen to add to the meal, with paper plates, napkins and such. Some sat at the table and some in the family room. Everyone appeared very congenial and at home. That's what Mom C always wanted. A Happy Family.

CHAPTER TWENTY-TWO

The church sanctuary was in splendor with colorful Christmas decorations. Waiting guests filled the pews, excited and eager for the wedding ceremony to begin. The parents and family guests have been seated. Organ music can be heard, as the excited crowd kept checking to see if the wedding party might be starting down the aisle at any time.

Soon the pastor stepped out of one of the doors in front of the sanctuary, followed by two young handsome men, dressed in black tuxes, with smiles on their faces. They were joined by Joe Torrey. The guys had asked Joe, their mechanic, to be their best man. The four men took their place in front of the congregation, then the wedding march started. Katelynn, dressed in her lovely red dress, was encouraged to walk slowly down the aisle. Her brother, Lamar, appearing so handsome in his suit, followed right behind, holding the lacy pillow carrying the two sets of rings. Every once in a while he would whisper (loudly) to his little sister to throw the rose petals from her basket. Terryli, the maid of honor for the girls, escorted by her new fiancé, were next. The two brides maids, dear friends of the twins, strolled slowly behind in their beautiful red dresses, escorted by two young men in dark suits, friends of Lance and Lyle. Then two beautiful brides dressed in the lovely gowns their Mother had designed were escorted in between their father to the front of the sanctuary, their smiling faces aglow.

Everyone was in their place.

The afternoon ceremony was very meaningful. The pastor's message encouraged each of the bridal couples how important it is to love, honor and respect each other along with being faithful, understanding and kind. God instituted the marriage of one man and one woman. We should honor our Christian commitments to God, as well as each other. He also encouraged those in attendance to renew their marriage vows between each other as man and woman, which God blesses and continues to bless.

A pleasant reception followed the ceremony in the fellowship hall. Every one congratulated, kissed and hugged the two couples, wishing them many years of happiness; also recognizing the parents and new members of the family. The huge decorated cake, featuring two couples, was cut and enjoyed by all. Thoughtful gifts were opened with enthusiasm.

The time was swiftly breezing away, since the four needed to be at the airport to catch their flights for the honeymooners. About that time, two gorgeous bouquets were thrown. A white limousine pulled up to the church, ready to load the suitcases that had been packed and ready to go for several days, and ready to carry the two couples away.

The girls quickly changed from their wedding gowns to comfortable pant suits. The guys changed to slacks, shirts and sport coats. Their families assured each one that they would be sure their clothes and gifts would be secured and in their new home when they returned from their honeymoon. The family and friends were soon hugging and saying their good byes. The huge car finally zoomed its way toward the airport.

After their bags were checked in at each location, Lance and Dawnelle to Hawaii and Lyle and Rochelle to New York, they had time to meet at one of the restaurants in the airport for coffee until Lyle and Rochelle needed to be at their gate, since they were first to leave.

Both couples were so excited. A new life was beginning. It seemed like everything they had ever done was together. Now one couple would be flying east to New York; the other couple west to Hawaii. The weather in New York would be cold. The weather in Hawaii was for swimsuits. They promised to call each other…well whenever they could. The time difference would be much different.

Finally, Lyle and Rochelle needed to be at their gate leaving for New York. The girls smiled with tears rolling down their cheeks. Both were thrilled, excited, and scared! Scared? A new life is to begin with the men they loved so much. As Christians, their wedding night would be one of sharing and learning. The girls were both virgins. They had learned their new husbands were also. Each one would be patient, and sure they would they be pleased with each other, as they expressed their love as husband and wife.

Mom had talked with her daughters about what to expect. Dad C had shared with the guys his view points on being a husband. Since Lance and Lyle's parents were dead, they respected the girl's parents, and were willing to listen and share their thoughts with their new father-in-law.

When Lyle and Rochelle arrived at the airport in New York, they retricved their luggage, then soon located a taxi to take them to the smaller airport. From there they would fly to the town closer to the Bed and Breakfast they had rented for their week near Niagra Falls.

Directions to the Inn had been given them at the car rental, along with a map of New York and some brochures. It was after midnight by the time they had rented a car and found the lovely old mansion in the woods in up-state New York. They both were thrilled after seeing the place where they would stay. The room was beautifully decorated with antiques and a queen sized canopy bed. There was a nice sized bathroom adjoining the bedroom, a sitting area with two comfortable chairs, and a sun porch surrounded with windows, which over looked a wooded area, but too dark to enjoy the view until morning.

The manager who showed them to the wedding suite, was very nice, and told them breakfast would be at eight in the morning. Then he smiled as he left the room.

The time being late, Rochelle opened up her small suitcase to find the her special negligee, and immediately groaned, "Oh, dear! I think I have Dawnelle's suitcase. I hope that's okay. We wear pretty much the same undies, make up, and such. I'd better check the large suitcase, too. Oh, no! This one has swimsuits and summer clothes." She began to giggle. "That means she has my warm clothes. I guess you know what we'll have to do tomorrow…go shopping," she grinned.

They both laughed.

He teased her about goofing up, even though it was Lyle who had carried the identical suitcases into the airport back in Seattle.

In the mean time, Lance and Dawnelle had arrived at the airport on the big island of Hawaii. They rented a car, and soon found their fantastic Bed and Breakfast overlooking Hilo Bay on the big Island. The Victorian mansion gave the appearance of a castle. Since it was night, it was romantically lit up with outdoor lighting.

"Oooo, such an ideal place for our honeymoon. Let's go swimming! It's so nice and warm outside," Dawnelle smiled dreamily. When she opened her suitcase, all she found were long sleeved blouses, sweaters, and warm pants. She began to laugh in astonishment, "Guess what? I have Rochelle's suitcase, so she must have mine. I don't think she'd need any of my swimsuits in New York this time of year, and I sure don't need her sweaters!"

"Well, we could go skinning dipping," Lance winked at her with a grin on his beaming face.

"I don't think so," Dawnelle shook her head, grinning. "I'm sure they'll have some swimsuits in the shops close by. But we'll have to wait until tomorrow to go shopping," she sang.

"I imagine we'll find something to do tonight," Lance still had that sexy grin on his face, as he winked his glorious blue eyes, lifting his eyebrows several times.

Morning came early, as the sun shown brightly through the window resting on Dawnelle's lovely face. When she opened her eyes, the first wonderful sight she saw was the smiling face of her phenomenal husband. It had been an enchanted night. Lance leaned over to give her a passionate kiss. They both smiled at each other, so much in love.

"Well, I guess we'd better get up and enjoy the majestic scenery I've heard so much about, Mrs. Taylor," Lance finally spoke.

"What a lovely name. I love it," Dawnelle said dreamily, then reached over and gave him a kiss.

"I'm starved. Let's go find out what kind of breakfast they're serving," Lance gave her another sweet kiss, then said, "Hmm, I'd better not do that again, or we'll be late for breakfast."

Dawnelle grinned and hurriedly jumped out of bed to claim the bathroom first. She quickly climbed into the huge tub to freshen up, dried herself in a lush towel, then put on the soft colorful kimono given to guests, while trying to figure out what to wear. She finally decided on Rochelle's brand new, blue, pant suit. Of course it fit perfectly.

Breakfast! What a delight! Rich Kona coffee, beautifully served fresh fruits of all kinds, macadamia nut granola, all served outside on the lanai, while overlooking swaying palm trees, blooming orchids and other tropical flowers, as well as the scenic bay. It was after breakfast when they decided to save the walk through the grounds until later in the evening. Instead, they wanted to drive around the island and see some of the sights. But first, Dawnelle decided they'd better stop in town, just a few blocks away, and find a swim suit.

The shops were just the action for tourists. Not only did they find plenty styles of swim suits, but beautiful Hawaiian designed dresses and shirts. Of course, Dawnelle had to buy a couple dresses and swim suits, and convinced Lance he needed a couple shirts and swim trunks. Then, they proceeded on to visit rainbow falls and Volcanoe's National Park.

In the meantime, another couple in New York had just climbed out of their plush bed. Their thoughts were equal to those of Lance and Dawnelle's. Love was growing. Over looking their glassed in balcony, the scenery was magical. It was located about fifteen minutes to the Falls, they were told.

"Let's go get some breakfast, then let's go scouting around," Lyle suggested.

"Okay, I'm so excited about seeing Niagra Falls. I've heard so much about how beautiful it is," Rochelle beamed.

There was seating in the dining room. Lyle and Rochelle

found a table close by the fireplace, after dishing up a variety of luscious foods. There was ham, Canadian bacon, sausage, eggs, anyway they wanted them cooked, plus Belgium waffles, pancakes, juices, just anything the taste buds would like. Breakfast was delicious and filling. They both stuffed themselves; then went back to their rooms, grabbed their coats, and before they headed out the door, one of the ladies called out, "Remember, there will be snacks and a variety of drinks available all day."

Lyle and Rochelle both grinned, and thanked them for the delightful news. It didn't take long before they heard the roaring sound of the falls cascading to the lake below. All of a sudden, there it was. Huge! Magnificent! Spectacular! The wonder of the impressive falls was in view. How powerful!

"I can't believe we're really here," Rochelle was overwhelmed. "Isn't this so exciting?"

"I'm so glad you are here with me, my love. I enjoy just seeing your beautiful face when it lightens up with joy. I hope we can always be so much in love, as we are this very minute," Lyle gazed at his lovely bride. Not carrying whether there was anyone around or not, he kissed her soft lips so passionately. Her response was equal to his. A couple walked by. The man whistled lightly.

Rochelle's face turned crimson.

They followed the well landscaped pathways for awhile, holding hands and just enjoying…being. No where else did they want to be right now…just together in this place God had created for the enjoyment of all His creation.

After viewing the falls from every angle they could see, and taking pictures of every site," Lyle said, "Let's go on the Canadian side of the falls. I've heard some say the view is even more spectacular."

They found a sightseeing bus close by. It not only crossed the bridge into Canada, but would take them to historic "Niagra on the Lake" in Ontario, which again was gorgeous and fun. Once again they exclaimed over the fantastic view of the falls. After awhile they decided to eat at the "Top of the Falls" restaurant for their main meal for the day, since they were stuffed again with delicious food, and knew they didn't need anymore food for a long time.

"Tomorrow we'd better do a little shopping. I need to buy some warmer clothes. Dawnelle's clothes were meant for Hawaii, not the east coast in the winter," Rochelle shivered as she spoke.

"Okay by me, my dear Mrs. Taylor," was Lyle's answer. "We'd better catch our tour bus back to New York and head for our cozy room. I sure don't want you catching a cold."

"Oh, I love the sound of that name," she grinned with her loving eyes, as well as her mouth. "Say it again."

"You like the name, "Mrs. Taylor"? I rather like it myself," Lyle beamed, then sealed it with a loving kiss.

Rochelle noticed a dress shop once they were back near their Inn. "Let's stop off here and see if you can find something warmer to wear, honey." Lyle suggested. There was some snuggly warm sweaters, so Lyle talked her into buying a couple. Also, a warm hat and gloves, looked enticing. She said she would buy them, if he would buy something. So, he found a sweater and a warm furry hat and gloves for himself. Now they both decided they could face the elements, whatever comes.

The following morning there was a light snow covering the ground around the large mansion. They were both glad they had taken time to go shopping the evening before. A little snow was not going to detour their venture. In fact, it was fun, as the tiny little flakes clung to their eyelashes, while taking a short walk around their home away from home, to enjoy the well kept gardens.

The Historic National Fort Niagra wasn't very far from their dwelling, so they decided it would be an interesting tour. After filling up with another delicious breakfast, they drove their rental car to visit the old Fort, a favorite place for sightseers. The Old Fort stands on a bluff overlooking Lake Ontario a short distance from Niagra Falls. It became a well known Fort in 1726, although it was in use before that time. Lyle was very interested in the history: the old buildings, old pictures, weapons, outfits and such. An important part of the Northern Continent in forming Canada and the United States…for Great Britain, France, and the Indians who dwelled in the area first.

Back in Hawaii Lance and Dawnelle were touring the Big Island by rental car. The tropical greenery and weather on the way to and around Rainbow Falls was warm and exciting. The falls was flowing full and swift. Divers were seen diving from off the top, which looked like fun to Lance but too daring for Dawnelle. She didn't feel she was a good enough swimmer. The leaves, on what we call house plants at home, were extremely large and growing wild snuggling within the trees. The tropical flowers were all so colorful and enormous. So many different colors and kinds of orchids were fantastic. Adjectives were very hard to come by, just trying to describe the beauty of the islands.

By night time, Dawnelle was dressed in one of her 'moo moo's,' and Lance in his floral Hawiian shirt for the Luau taking place in just a few minutes. They were sitting alongside the long table with many other guests. Sunset was spreading it's oranges and gold colors across the heavens, as the Hawaiian dancers were preparing to swing and sway to the beautiful Hawaiian music. The aroma of the roasting pig began to liven up the atmosphere. What a romantic way to arouse the emotions, as the dancers began to sway their hula dances to the lovely Hawaiian music.

Following the luau, fireworks began to light up the heavens, as everyone was anxious to welcome in the New Year. Three…two…one…the music claimed the atmosphere in joyful song as everyone was hugging and kissing their loved ones, while shouting out Happy New Year!

The fire works over Niagra Falls, as well as the nightly illumination of the Falls, was such a lovely way to close such a special evening for another young couple sharing their honeymoon in New York. "What a wonderful way to welcome in the New Year," Lyle and Rochelle exclaimed as they sealed their feelings in a warm kiss.

The next stop for the Taylors was an exciting visit to Kilauea Caldera Volcano and Observatory, then on to Halemaumau Crater. The sulfur in the air was rather chocking to the lungs, but impressive to be able to walk so close to something 'so alive.' Now, they decided it was time to be heading back to Hilo and their lovely room in the 'castle.'

The following day they went to see the Butterfly Conservatory. There were so many different kinds and colors of butterflies. It was so amazing. Some would land on Dawnelle's shoulders, in her hair, on Lance's nose. It was so much fun.

Picture taking was a must. They were so glad for the digital cameras they both had, which could take so many pictures, and be able to delete those you didn't want. "We must have hundreds of pictures to share with our family when we get home," Dawnelle exclaimed. "And we're only half way finished with our tour of Hawaii."

A trip by plane to the Island of Kauai was next on the agenda for our Hawaiian couple. They took a cruise along the river to the Fern Grotto, really feeling they were in a tropical jungle. Everywhere they went Hawaiian music was being played. The Hawaiian Love Song was a favorite. Waimea Canyon was another must to see. It's known as "The Grand Canyon of the Pacific." Even if you've seen the Grand Canyon in Arizona, this one is nearly as beautiful to see, the young couple decided. The colors are gorgeous and scenery is awesome. Maybe not 'quite' as big.

The last day in Hawaii, Lance and Dawnelle had to take one more swim in the warm waters surrounding the Big Island. They both had put on their new swimsuits before they left the lovely Inn. A drive along the rugged coast, sparkling like diamonds caught by the sun, soon found them a quiet place where they could pull over and take a swim. Palm trees swayed and whispered in the rustling wind, as the two enjoyed the refreshing warmth of the Pacific Ocean. Birds chirped in the trees close by, while brightly colored butterflies could be seen flying from one blossom to another. Truly a paradise, quiet and relaxing.

Dawnelle spoke softly, as she lie floating on her back thinking about Lance and her life ahead. "These memories we are making will be cherished forever. What a wonderful life we are going to have, My Love. I want you to know, whatever lies ahead for us, whether good or bad, I will always love you."

"My precious, Dawnelle, you and I, and any children we will have, will always be a blessing to me. With God as our guide, and Head of our Lives, I feel I am so very blessed already that you have become my wife. I love you, Mrs. Lance Taylor." They sealed their promise with a salty kiss. The sun was slowly descending over the rippling water, leaving streams of corals and golds spreading across the darkening sky.

Lyle and Rochelle were reminiscing, already, about their activities in wonderful New York.

Their flight in the small plane to New York City, and then on to Washington State and home would begin early in the morning. It was kinda sad, and yet, thinking about moving into their wonderful home they had decorated with love was waiting for their return, to really begin their new life together. As they shared their thoughts that night, how could anyone as much in love as they were, ever feel sad. Yes, they knew life isn't perfect. Problems will come. But, together, with God's direction, they will be able to face any challenge that will come their way. That was their prayer, as they sealed it with a kiss.

The phone began to ring.

"Hello," Rochelle answered.

"It's me, Dawnelle. Just wanted to say hi, and see you tomorrow. Sure do hope you and my new brother have had as wonderful a time as Lance and I have had."

"Hi, Sis. Oh, yes. We've had a marvelous time here in fantastic New York. We've taken so many pictures. I hope you have, too."

"Millions!" Dawnelle laughed. "We'll have so much fun seeing each other's photos. It's hard to leave, and yet we're excited about going to 'our' home in Washington."

"Yes, we've talked about that, too," Rochelle agreed.

They went on and talked for a while, the guys and the girls. Then decided who ever got to the airport first would wait for the other couple. While waiting they would call their parents. When everyone arrived at the airport, they would then take the shuttle bus to their own home, the Bed and Breakfast. The following day they would go see their parents. That settled, they said their good-byes.

CHAPTER TWENTY-THREE

Both Taylor couples have been home from their honeymoons for a couple days. Their first night together in the big home was exciting, and very late. How thankful they were that Mom had made sure everything was clean and in place. Beds were all freshly made up, after all the company left and had shared how much they enjoyed their stay in the Bed and Breakfast. Dad had placed each wedding gift on the dining room table, or near it, for the girls to find a special place for each gift.

Mom had made a special dinner the following night at the Collin's home, preparing all the favorite foods she could remember each one enjoyed. The two couples hugged their mother and thanked her for such a thoughtful and delicious meal, and for all she and Dad had done to make sure their home was in good shape after all the company.

Now it was time for the twins to share. Dawnelle and Lance had bought Mom and Dad colorful shirts and dresses from Hawaii, as well as for Rochelle and Lyle. Rochelle had bought a DVD of Niagra Falls. Lyle had to have one of historic Old Fort

Nisqually, which they had both enjoyed. He even bought one of the warm, furry hats for his new Dad. They also bought T shirts with a picture of Niagra Falls for each one. Everyone was so thankful for the digital cameras. They viewed the photos of each couples honeymoon on the TV screen in the family room. Some of the photos were silly, causing a lot of jovial teasing.

During their conversations that evening, Rochelle brought to their attention the need to name their Bed and Breakfast. Dawnelle quickly agreed. They also needed to work up a brochure to start advertising their B & B on the website. Many thoughtful suggestions were mentioned. Finally, they decided to name their lovely home, Mountain View Inn, since nearly every eastern window proclaimed a glorious view of the Cascade mountains, with Mt. Rainier reigning above all. Rochelle volunteered to work on a brochure the following day. They all agreed that it should include the Taylor Helicopter Sightseeing Tours as part of the attraction for customers of both businesses.

At dinner one night, Lance looked at Dawnelle with concern in his eyes, "Have you noticed your Dad lately?"

"Now that you mention it, yes. He hasn't been as cheerful and talkative as he usually is. I hope there isn't anything wrong?"

"We'd better find out," Rochelle said.

"Let's have the folks over for dinner tomorrow night," Lyle suggested.

They all agreed.

Although it was a cold evening, it was so nice when Mom and Dad rang the doorbell the following evening, then opened the door upon hearing, "Come in." The girls were so excited, since it would be their first meal prepared in their home for Mom and Dad.

A pleasant aroma drifted from the kitchen. "It sure smells good in here. My taste buds are overflowing, telling my stomach, 'I want to eat.'" Dad grinned, as he entered the kitchen, followed by Mom C. In her hands was a plate of her famous crescent rolls snuggled under a cheerful kitchen towel.

"Come sit down here, Dad," Lyle pulled out a chair from the table. "How are two of my favorite people today?"

"We're all right. I'll bet you youngun's have been keeping plenty busy," Dad smiled.

"Yes. Since we started advertising our Inn, we've had several phone calls asking about it. One couple has made reservations to spend a week-end in just a couple of weeks. "I'm so thrilled. They will be our first paying couple," Rochelle shared with excitement.

"The guys are just about finished with building the hanger, shop and office. Marina Arnold is anxious to move into the office and get it ready for use. She's so pleased that it will be about five miles closer for her to drive to work," Dawnelle shared.

"How's the Collins' Cosmetic Company doing, Dad?" Lance asked.

"We manage to keep busy. The new products Dawnelle helped create have really given the business quite a boost. In fact, there's been a couple of the major cosmetic companies interested in wanting to buy us out." Mr. C's facial expression didn't show much pleasure in his statement. Then he went on, "Too many times larger companies are jealous of the competition of we smaller companies, and try to cause trouble. I don't think I'm ready to give up my position yet."

"Surely they can't force you to sell," Lyle stated.

"No. This is still a free country, but they can make it difficult sometimes. I've decided to talk with my attorney and see what

I need to do. Some people just don't understand what 'No' means.

"Is this why you have been so quiet lately, dear?" Mrs. C eyed her husband so sadly.

"I don't like to bring my problems home to you, Love. Things will work out for the good. God has always been such a blessing to us. We just need to trust Him. This sure has been a tasty dinner. Now, let's have some dessert. I'm sure one of my daughters must have baked me an angel food cake," he grinned, wanting to change his families thoughts to happier ones.

"May I set up for us to see our DVD on Old Fort Nisqually?" Lyle asked, as the girls left the table to prepare the dessert.

Everyone agreed, with a fancy plate of angel food cake piled high with whipped cream, they made their way to the TV room where they enjoyed the historic movie and scenery, which of course led into watching the movie on Niagra Falls.

Grant Collins hasn't been feeling well for several days. Part of his trouble, he knew, was the stress from the constant calls from a major company seriously interested in taking over Collins' Cosmetic Company. At first, it was rather flattering to have a company so well thought of interested. But now, the persistent calls wanting him to sell was causing him to feel perturbed, as well as frustrated. He wasn't sleeping through the night, having to get up in the middle of a restless sleep with pain in his back, then he found blood in his urine. Finally, he decided to see his doctor with the urinary problem. He didn't want to alarm his wife or family until he discovered if the cause might be something serious.

After a welcome greeting from the doctor he had befriended several years ago, he was examined and the doc heard his concerns. The doctor decided to schedule Grant for some tests. One was the prostate specific antigen (PSA) test. Also, he said to report back to see him as soon as they received notice of the results from all the tests. In the mean time, he suggested some over the counter medicine for the pain and sleepless nights.

A few days later, in the doctor's office with the test reports in hand, it revealed Grant has prostatitus, a painful infection of the prostrate. The doctor said he must cut down on spicy foods, no caffeine, and to eat more high-fiber foods, and to drink lots of fluids during the day, especially lots of water, but less water at bedtime. He prescribed some antibiotics for the infection. "Sometimes a good old hot bath helps soothe the pain, and reduce your stress. If the pelvic pain or urinary problems suddenly get worse, then make another appointment. Even though you said there is no known problems of prostrate cancer in your family, we still want regular monitoring, in case more aggressive treatment may be needed. Remember, prostrate cancer in older men grows slowly, but if found early, it can often be cured." The Doctor explained.

On his way home, Grant felt relieved with the news, and glad for such a caring doctor. Now he felt comfortable sharing with his family what the doctor had told him. The family was sorry he had not mentioned his concerns earlier. They felt he should not have gone through the added stress all alone.

Dawnelle wasn't feeling very well when she got up one morning shortly after learning of her father's health problems. She barely made it to the bathroom, when she lost what little breakfast she had eaten. Since it was flu season, she felt that was probably what was wrong with her, and hoped she could curtail the bug before the rest of the family caught it. Each one of the family members had received flu shots before Christmas. However, she found some flu medicine in the medicine cabinet, so decided to take some. By early afternoon she was feeling better.

Their first couple to spend a week-end in their Inn was due tomorrow. A breakfast menu was planned for the three days. It was going to be very special. Mom had given them some of her ideas and recipes to practice on their husbands during the week. Of course the house was ready for visitors. The weather was trying to cooperate; cold but sunny was the weatherman's report.

Rochelle was surprised when she answered the knock on the front door the next morning. Their expectation was to find a younger couple staying with them in the Inn. This couple was closer to their parent's age. Both were full of smiles.

"Come in. Come in to Mountain View Inn. It's so good to have you, Mr. & Mrs. Carlson. We hope you will enjoy your stay with us," Rochelle greeted them.

Unfortunately, Dawnelle was in the bathroom, giving up her breakfast…again. Pretty soon she came into the room with a smile on her pale face.

"Oh, honey, are you all right?" Concern was shown on Mrs. Carlson's face.

"I just can't seem to keep anything down. I won't get too close to you. I don't think I'm contagious, but no need to take any chances. Rochelle, would you mind showing our guests up to their room, then I'll show them around when they get settled? I'm sure I'll be all right by then."

"Of course, I'll be glad to show our guests to their room," Rochelle smiled at the couple. "We'll let you choose which room you want, since you're our only guests for the week-end. In fact, you are our first guests to stay in our Bed and Breakfast. So, if we forget anything, please let us know. We're very excited you chose to stay with us." Rochelle called Lyle to help take their luggage upstairs. He was in the kitchen getting a cup of coffee.

Before Lyle and Mr. Carlson went to get their luggage from their car, Mr. Carlson introduced his wife as Amy and his name as Martin. They told them this was their first stay in a Bed and Breakfast, and was looking forward to such a lovely home to spend their little vacation in. While the men went to the car, Amy glanced all around the living room and dining room, admiring all the lovely antiques, and the beautiful chandelier hanging over the dining table. She couldn't wait to see their bedroom upstairs.

They chose the bedroom with the pale green, antique furniture. The room was a dream come true to Amy. She had always admired antiques.

Martin and Amy were newly weds, Amy shared with Rochelle and Lyle with a shy smile on her face. She looked lovingly at her new husband. He grinned at her and gently stole a kiss.

Martin explained, with a slight southern accent, that they are on their honeymoon. They both had been married before, but their spouses had both died several years ago. "I didn't ever want to get married again, but when I met Amy through a friend, I fell in love with her with the first glance. My friend had spoken so well of her. But he hadn't prepared me for her beauty. She kept turning me down every time I'd ask her to marry me. But, after several months of determination, I finally won out," he gave her a loving smile.

She shyly looked up into his eyes, then said, "I thought he was so handsome. I couldn't imagine him wanting to marry me."

"Congratulations! How exciting!" Rochelle exclaimed. "Lyle and I, and our twin siblings, Dawnelle and Lance, have only been married a couple months. This is our new adventure, opening a Bed and Breakfast. The guys have moved their

Helicopter business on the back of our property. They have a sightseeing business, if you might be interested in seeing Washington by air," she added with a smile.

"Oh, that would really be a treat," Amy looked at her husband with a grin and sparkling eyes.

"Anything you want, my love," Martin grinned at his lovely wife. His eyes were a deep blue. His hair had a touch of silver around the sides. He was in top shape for his age. Amy was slim and trim, with auburn hair styled in a short, appealing cut. They made a very attractive couple.

Dawnelle spoke. "We plan on showing you a wonderful time while you are here. I forget, where are you from?"

"We're from Atlanta, Georgia. We've never been in the Northwest before. We thought it might be a nice area to visit on our 'out of the ordinary' trip," Martin explained.

"Well, Lance and I will take you around in our helicopter as our wedding gift to you. Would you both like to go for a cruise in the air?" Lyle asked.

"Oh, why don't we all go? Dawnelle and I haven't been flying with you guys for a long time," Rochelle suggested.

"If I can keep my stomach quiet for awhile," Dawnelle said, making a silly face.

"Well, let's get Martin and Amy situated for today, and tomorrow after breakfast we'll all go for a ride, viewing the great, evergreen state of Washington. How does that sound to everyone?" Lance had come in from outside during the middle of the conversation.

Martin and Amy whole heartily agreed. They decided they would just relax for awhile today. It would be nice just to roam around the yard and enjoy the peace and quiet, as well as the beautiful scenery right here for the rest of the day. Lyle mentioned he would give them directions to a very nice restaurant not far from the Inn, for the evening meal. Dawnelle showed them the bookcase in the dining room with some popular books, if they would be interested in reading.

"Please make yourselves at home," both girls said at once with a grin.

The couple went up to their bedroom. The other two couples went about their work.

CHAPTER TWENTY-FOUR

Saturday was beautiful, with puffy white clouds spreading through the sky. A brisk breeze freshened the air. Breakfast was yummy, with Belgium waffles and homemade syrup, ham and eggs, lots of hot Seattle's Best coffee. Everyone was cheerful and ready for the scenic helicopter ride to begin as soon as the dishwasher was filled...and Dawnelle excused herself for a little trip to the bathroom. She still felt a little nauseated, but didn't want to be left behind.

Amy took Dawnelle aside for a few minutes, while the others waited on the back porch. "I am a RN, a registered nurse. Is there anything I can do to help you, honey? Do you think you might be pregnant? You seem to have the symptoms."

Dawnelle's dark brown eyes turned into huge brown eyes. She looked at Amy, then said, "Do you think so? I never even thought about that. Her mouth turned into a grin, then she tried to muffle a scream. Rochelle hurried into the dining area of the kitchen, where the other two ladies were hugging each other.

"What in the world is going on?" She asked.

"Dawnelle began to laugh, "Amy thinks I may be pregnant!"

Rochelle grabbed her sister, hugging, and exclaiming how wonderful.

"We should get you a pregnancy test to see for sure. Then you really need to make an appointment with your doctor," Amy encouraged her. "You'll need to get into prenatal care soon, so you can have a healthy baby," she smiled.

"This is so exciting. Should I tell Lance, or wait until I find out for sure?" Dawnelle contemplated, looking at Amy.

"You'll have to decide that for yourself. He may feel left out if you wait to tell him," Amy considered, "but sometimes it's more fun after you find out for sure first."

Just then, Lance came into the dinning room. "Hey, what's going on here? I thought we were going to take a ride," he grinned, then looked at his sweet wife. "Are you all right, honey?"

"Yes. I…uh…we were just talking. We're ready to go. Does everyone have a jacket? It may get cold before we return home," Dawnelle smiled, shyly. "I'd better go get me one."

"Why don't you grab some crackers. Sometimes something a little salty helps that tummy," Amy suggested.

Soon everyone was situated comfortably in the helicopter, raring to go. Lyle was the pilot today. He directed the chopper right over Mt. Rainier, which stood out so fascinating, so full of glistening snow. It makes you want to reach out and touch it, someone said.

From over the mountain other high peaks in the Cascade Range could be seen. Rochelle put names to the ones that were visible, saying the first thing each morning when she gets up is look out the window to check on 'her' mountain. Grandpa always told her to go take a bite out of the ice cream cone over there.

Martin had heard about the eruption of Mt. St. Helens back in 1980, and asked if it would be safe to fly over that mountain. Amy was very agreeable to that. Lyle said, "sure."

Rochelle informed them, " It had been such an almost perfectly shaped mountain before it erupted. Our grandparents had taken many pictures of the mountain, and often fished in the lake at it's foot. Although quite a lot of snow, St. Helens isn't as grand a shape as it was.

"Still, it well be fun to tell our friends we flew over Mt. St. Helens." Amy shared her thoughts.

After viewing St. Helens, they flew on west to see the Pacific ocean and the Coast Range of mountains, where Mt. Olympus stood proud and in charge, before heading back to the Seattle area. There were many ships at the docks in the Puget Sound waters downtown. The Space Needle stood out grand and tall. It had been built for the World's Fair back in the early 1960's, and is still a favorite place to visit when in downtown Seattle. There are two restaurants circling the Space Needle. The view from either one makes sightseeing Seattle, the many islands in the blue waters of Puget Sound, and of course the mountains most Northwesterners are so proud of such a delight.

"We'd better be heading back home. I'm sure everyone is getting hungry," Lyle expressed.

"I think it would be nice if Amy and I took all of us out to dinner this evening. Would that be agreeable to everyone?" Martin suggested.

"Oh, that would be so nice," Amy agreed with her husband. "Let's go some place special where I can wear my new dress I bought for our trip."

"Super! A dress up dinner. That would be fun," Dawnelle said in agreement.

"Why don't we go Dutch treat?" Rochelle offered.

"No, no. Dinner will be on me," Martin insisted with a smile. Amy shook her head in agreement.

"I know a nice place not far from home that has a wonderful menu, plus a lovely lady plays the piano and sings 50's and 60's music," Lance stated.

"Okay by me," Lyle joined in.

The evening passed by very quickly, and very special. At the steak house, they sat by a window overlooking a lush garden. Even a few crocus were peaking through the well maintained garden, even though it was mostly of evergreen bushes. The Black Angus steaks nearly melted in their mouths, because they were so tender. Lyle had mentioned to the matre'd that this was a honeymoon dinner for all three couples, so for dessert he brought each couple a huge stemmed, dessert dish of vanilla ice cream smothered with strawberries (grown in the Puyallup Valley, he stressed), and topped with whipped cream. Each couple was to share the luscious dessert.

"I think my stomach has expanded at least five inches," Amy groaned. The ladies all agreed with their new friend, as the guys had to end up finishing the rest of the delicious dessert.

While driving back to the Inn, Amy asked if there was a church close by to their home. Lyle mentioned that they could visit their church tomorrow with them, if they would like. The older couple was very pleased, and said they would like it very much.

Rochelle shared that their singing group would be singing a special medley tomorrow for the church special, and would need to practice their song one more time tonight before bedtime.

"That would be lovely," Martin and Amy sounded very pleased.

"Would it be all right if we listened while you practice?" Amy asked.

"Of course. Just don't pay any attention to any errors we make," Dawnelle laughed.

"We're so thrilled you would like to visit our church with us. You'll get to meet Rochelle's and my parents. Mother plays the piano for us when we sing, and Dad sings bass in our singing group." Dawnelle informed them.

"It's been a wonderful day and a lovely beginning for our marriage. Thank you so much for letting us stay in your Bed and Breakfast, as well as the inspiring trip in the helicopter," Martin's features shown how much he enjoyed such a special day.

Everyone agreed, since it was getting late, they'd better practice the special music and head toward bed, as soon as they can once at home.

Dawnelle mentioned she would like to stop at the pharmacy first, on the way home. It only took a few minutes, since Amy helped her locate the item she wanted. The two couples practiced the song they were to sing the following morning. Martin and Amy stayed to listen and were so enthused over such a professional rendition of the music. They thanked them and headed up the stairs to their room. Amy quickly turned around before she reached the top of the stairs and asked Dawnelle if she needed any help with her new project. But, they had found time to discuss the process together before saying their good nights, so Dawnelle felt she could handle it.

A few minutes later, everyone in the house heard a yell! "We're pregnant!" Lance's deep voice could be heard throughout the house. Everyone joined together at the bottom of the stairs. The three women grabbing each other, hugging.

The men shaking hands, hugging, and congratulating the 'pregnant' couple. It would be a long time before anyone got some sleep tonight. It was a 'supercalalistic' day!

"Oh, I know it is late, but I've just got to call Mama and Daddy," Dawnelle expressed.

Some more squealing, took place when Mom's sleepy voice heard the news over the phone. Then Dad grabbed the phone from Mom to find out what all the ruckus was about, and he began to express his excitement.

"We're going to be grandparents!" Both joyfully burst out the words together. After hanging up the phone, they hugged each other. Mom with tears in her eyes. Dad's face was full of happiness.

"Our little girl is going to give us a grand child. How wonderful."

Mom kissed her dear husband in agreement.

Sunday, the Carlson's followed the Taylor couples to church in their own car. The Carlson's decided during breakfast that they wanted to explore downtown Seattle after church. They had heard about Pike's Place Fish Market, and the tour of underground Old Seattle, etc. They had planned to leave Monday for sight seeing in British Columbia, then head back to Atlanta.

The Taylor twins were anxious to visit with their parents. They didn't have much time to talk with them all week. After the news of the expecting couple, Mom just had to see and hug her daughters. She hadn't been able to sleep but a very few hours all last night, she said. So, of course, she fixed a delicious dinner, and invited the two couples over to share all the news of the past week.

Have you thought of names? Do you want a boy or a girl? You're going to need a baby crib and all the things a baby needs.

We'll have to plan a baby shower. On and on Mom spoke of her coming plans…so excited.

Dawnelle started to giggle, "Mom, we really need to go to the doctor for a confirmation on the home pregnancy test I took. Amy Carlson, our B & B guest, is a nurse. It looks pretty certain that I'm pregnant, but she feels I still need our doctor's confirmation.

"You'll have to call him tomorrow for an appointment." Mom's voice was very firm.

Dawnelle laughed. "I think you're even more excited than I am."

Mom's face turned crimson. "I'm sorry, hun. I guess I am. I just love you so much."

"Don't you love me?" Rochelle made a silly face.

"Of course, Darling. I'm sorry for leaving you out. Your turn will come soon, I'm sure. We will be equally thrilled when it happens, as we are now for your sister and her husband."

It was hard to say good-bye to the Carlson's on Monday after a hearty breakfast. They had been such a sweet couple, also, a lot of fun on their adventures together. But, they were starting a new life as newly weds. They said they hoped they could spent next year's anniversary at the Mountain View Inn, Bed and Breakfast. After all the hugs and good-byes, the couple drove away, Amy waving and Martin honking.

Dawnelle couldn't get in to see her doctor until Wednesday. Everyone was on pins and needles until she come home Wednesday afternoon. Rochelle and their mother were with Dawnelle, when she went in to see the doctor at the office.

Lance was waiting at the door, when they returned to the Inn. "Are we pregnant?" was his first words.

Dawnelle slowly looked into his eyes. She didn't say a word.

"Wel-l-l?" Lance's face showed a concerned look.

Then Dawnelle started laughing, "Yes! We are pregnant. However, it's too soon to take an ultra sound to tell what sex it is. Do we really want to know?" She asked.

"Hmm, we'll have to think about that," he grinned.

"It would be fun to know, wouldn't it? Then we can buy little boys things...or little girls things," Rochelle thought out loud.

About that time Lyle had come in the house. "What's going on. Am I going to be an uncle or not?" He couldn't help laughing.

"Yes, my love. We're going to be aunt and uncle in about seven months," Rochelle, smiling, shared with her husband.

"I need to get on home." Mom interrupted the conversation. "I'll call your dad at work and share the news from there. Bye now. You get plenty of rest. If you need any help, just give me a call." She hugged Dawnelle, along with the rest of her special loved ones.

A busy week followed. Dawnelle was feeling much better. Morning sickness didn't last all day now, just once in a while. She was cleaning up the kitchen, when she noticed Rochelle was looking a little peeked. "Are you feeling all right, Sis?"

"Well, to be honest, I've been kinda nauseated for the last couple days. But I'll get over it pretty soon."

A smile began to spread across Dawnelle's face.

"What's so funny?" Rochelle didn't think there was anything to be funny about.

"Let's go to the drug store. I want to buy you something." Dawnelle tried to look serious.

"I really don't feel like it. But okay, if you're buying," she groaned.

"I'll be just a minute, if you don't want to go in," Dawnelle gave her sister a hug.

When they got back home, Rochelle was taken into the bathroom downstairs. Dawnelle opened up the bag and gave the 'gift' to her sister.

"When Rochelle read what was on the box, she glanced at her sister and said, "Oh. You think I might beeee..."

"Let's find out," Dawnelle grinned.

"I can't wait till I tell Lyle," Rochelle almost screamed after taking the test. "He was so disappointed that you and Lance got pregnant first."

They both laughed. Thrilled...they both felt so good.

"Do you want to call and make an appointment first?"

"I probably should, but I don't know if I can keep it a secret," Rochelle spoke.

"Let's make an appointment, then we'll go out to the chopper hanger and find the guys," Dawnelle suggested.

The appointment was made for Thursday. The girls grabbed a jacket and made their way out to the hanger. They couldn't find the guys, but knew they had to be around some place, since both helicopters were there. Finally, they found their men in the office, going over some papers with Joe and Marina. They all looked up when they went in the door.

"Wow. To what do we owe this occasion. Both of our lovely wives are here," Lance spoke teasingly. The wives very seldom went out to see them at work. During the day they usually saw them at lunch time at the house. They hugged each other, said hi to the two employees, then Rochelle told them she had some news.

Joe and Marina offered to step outside, but Rochelle said to please stay. They could hear what she had to say.

Rochelle then spoke, shyly. "I think I have some news. I won't know for sure until Thursday when I see the doctor."

"What's wrong, darling? Are you sick?" Lyle's face turned an instant white.

"I have been sick lately. Dawnelle told me to make an appointment to see the doctor, but she did give me a test to take, and it showed yes." She glanced up to him.

"You'll be okay, sweetheart. I'll take care of you, whatever it is," Lyle grabbed his wife and hugged her.

"I'm so glad you said you will help. 'Cause a lot of wives say their husbands don't like to get up in the middle of the night to help." She was having fun with this explanation.

"Well, I'm not one of them. Now tell me, what do you think might be wrong with you? It's not cancer, or anything like that." Lyle's concern was so sweet.

"No. It's not cancer, I'm sure. But it could hurt a little," she couldn't hide a slight grin.

"Oh, Rochelle, put the man out of his misery," snickering, Dawnelle couldn't keep her voice quiet anymore.

"My dear husband," Rochelle began, "We may join Dawnelle and Lance about the same time as their little one comes. We're pregnant! Oops, I probably shouldn't say that for sure, but we are pretty sure we are going to have a baby, too."

Wouldn't you know it! Lyle passed right out...flat on the floor. Lance tried to catch him, but he was all doubled over from laughing.

When Thursday come, Lance, Lyle, Dawnelle, Mom and Dad, and oh yes, Rochelle was at the doctor's office. The doctor came out of the office with Rochelle. Neither one had a smile on their face. The other five stood up to hear the news. The doctor knew each member of the Collins' family, since he had been the one to take care of the twins when they were born. Finally he spoke. "Are you folks all ready for the news?"

"Your daughter, maybe I should say…daughters are both pregnant. Now, before you say a word, please sit down.

Everyone was all ears!

"I've been checking over both of the girls records, and I believe both of your girls are going to have twins," he slowly grinned, then laughed.

Mom and Dad looked at each other beaming. Dad let out a war whoop!

The girls were both assisting their husbands that laid on the floor. "You'll be all right, honey." They both were kissing their sweethearts and cooing to them.

EPILOGUE

It has been three busy years since we have peeked into the lives of the Collins and Taylor families. Many things have taken place. Grant Collins has sold the Collins Cosmetic Company. With a lot of prayer from he and his wife, as well as the Taylor twins, they have purchased the Mountain View Inn, Bed and Breakfast, from the Taylor families. All concerned, they decided it was a good, healthy and financial move.

The Bed and Breakfast, along with the men's Helicopter Sight Seeing Tours business, has been thriving. Leslie has been in her glory, since she has taken on the job of welcoming guests into their home, and using her cooking skills in preparing the meals. Not only does she prepare a gourmet breakfast for the guests at the Mountain View Inn, but has added a dinner on Friday nights for guests with reservations only, since their seating is limited. Following the dinners, the Easy Listening Five put on a concert. Sometimes the five grandchildren join in the singing…a little off key at times, but always a big attraction.

Yes, there are five grandchildren. Dawnelle and Lance have

three children...triplets...John (Johnny), Joseph (Joey) and Jamie. Jamie is the only grand daughter of the bunch. Rochelle and Lyle have twin boys: Joshua (Josh) and Jeremy. The boys all have dark curly hair like their daddy's, two have blue eyes and two have brown eyes. Jamie, the only girl, is the head of the pack most of the time. She thinks she should be in charge of all the antics, the boys complain. At least she says she doesn't cause the trouble, but with two brothers and two male cousins, she just can't seen to win! They always say she acts like a tiger, but she really acts like a pussy cat. She is a cute little blond, like her mother and aunt, but has blue eyes like her daddy.

Grant Collins has enjoyed his change in work habits. No more suits and ties. Levi's and sport shirts are his attire these days. And, he loves it. Leslie likes to have fresh fruits and vegetables for her meals, so Grant has been the gardener, and the caretaker of the fruit trees. With the help of a large sit down type lawn mower...big enough for rides for a couple little ones at a time...he takes care of the lawns.

Dawnelle and Rochelle have been helpers at the Inn. They help Mom with the laundry, cleaning rooms and just being available when needed. Otherwise, they are busy taking care of their own beautiful homes. Both Taylor families have similar large, sprawling, log homes built on an acre of land each, adjacent to their parents home, the Inn. Their homes are just opposite in design. Both have extra wide driveways that adjoin to the parking of the Bed & Breakfast, so it gives visitors to the Inn plenty of parking space. All of their homes have a view of the mountains, the creek flowing by, and the fascinating colors of sunrise and sunsets.

Papa Collins had a 'jungle gymn' set put up in his backyard. It consists of slides, a trampoline, a major sized swing set, and handle bars to crawl all over. He insists it's not only for his grandchildren, but also for the children of the Bed and Breakfast families to enjoy. So far, the children have always played well together. Of course, there are always squabbles, when you get little ones together. But, Papa is very pleased at how well mannered most of the children are. Little Jamie makes sure everyone get's along fine. However, her two brothers and two cousins don't always think she should be the boss. She may be a cutie, some people say, but to the others, she's still just the little squirt. Some people may think the children are spoiled. Papa just says they are well loved and very blessed.